BERNADETTE O'CONNOR

Let's Go Home

FINDING THERE WHILE STAYING HERE

National Library of Australia Cataloguing-in-Publication data:
Let's Go Home/Bernadette O'Connor
Fiction

ISBN: (sc) 978-0-6482304-8-9
ISBN: (e) 978-0-6482304-7-2

Kokoda, Lucia and Xavier
Shine your light in the world every day.
Believe in your power to make a difference.
Remember that anything is possible.
So, Dream Big my babes.

CONTENTS

THERE, HIM

Lying in the bed, thoughts tumbled through my mind. *What was that? Who was that? Where was that?* I tried desperately to silence them, to be in the moment, one more time. *Seriously, what was that?*

I wanted to feel it again. I looked at him lying next to me. I dared not touch him. Yet, every fibre of my being wanted to touch him and feel it all over again. I knew if I went there my need may never stop. Did he feel it too? Surely, he must have. How could he not? I was struggling in this extraordinary and bizarre situation. *Seriously, what the fuck was that?* I desperately rummaged for an answer.

It all started, the night before. Now, it felt like

lifetimes ago. I snuggled into the comforting memory of what it felt like to be *there* again. That is all I wanted.

Yesterday morning, everything was different. Everything was normal, like a nothingness sort of normal. A normal I had grown accustomed to. A normal that everyone around me had accepted and embraced as enough. It was enough. Until now. When had I begun to accept my life, as enough? I felt an instant pain. When had I lost the feeling of knowing that there was more? That there is more than the emptiness all those around me seemingly slipped into.

Stop! Just stop it.

My life is fine just as it is. I'm fine. These are just untamable thoughts that were released in the ectasy of last night. And yet, I knew last night was real—surreal. Now, it both scared and excited me.

Yesterday evening, I had left the slopes after an extraordinary day skiing. I was alone. I had space to breathe and the freedom to fly down the slopes effortlessly. I was free to be whatever, wherever, whomever I chose to be. Nobody knew I was here. I had spontaneously jumped in the car and headed for the mountains. I needed space from my mum, my friends, from studying and life. My mum would presume that I was at a friend's house and I wasn't going to tell her any different. Some things can't be explained and some things *are* worth it. I knew that getting away for a day, was a non-negotiable, something was about to explode if I didn't find space. And so, I did.

I felt exuberant and alive as I walked into the bar for a warm drink before I drove home. Alive. I felt alive again, for the first time in years.

And then our eyes met.

∞

She caught my eye as she walked into the bar, she exuded joy. She had an aliveness in her expression, a dancing spirit in her eyes and the flush to her cheeks. I could not stop staring, like a magnet, I was drawn to her. Never had I seen or felt what I felt in that moment. It was completely overwhelming and frightening in its intensity. Until, the moment our eyes connected and the overwhelm vanished. There was no fear. I knew she felt it too, as she gasped and paused before taking a step towards me.

As she moved closer, there was a familiarity to her that I could not quite place. As she approached me, in some way, I could hear her thoughts as clearly as if they were my own.

What am I doing, seriously what am I doing? Oh, Dear God, I can't. I can't go to him. What is happening? And then, she stood in front of me. Her hands shook. I took her hands and as she looked into my eyes, she knew. She knew, as I did, that it was okay. But that didn't stop my head screaming. *What the hell is going on? What are you doing? This must stop! This must not stop.* My mind and soul battled for control. It was not the first time that I had experienced this inner conflict between what I should do and what my core being told me to do.

I looked deeply into her eyes—her soul—it was like a rod of lightning smashing through my body in the most incredible way. My head tried to make sense of what was going on, and my thoughts persisted, *How was I here, doing this, in this moment, with this girl?*

Three months ago, I came here to work on the ski slopes and get away from everything. To find and reclaim my space. To figure myself out. It's not that I didn't love Sam, my girlfriend. I did but I felt smothered and knew that something was not right. Out of my love for her, I gave myself and our relationship space, so that I could regroup, recalibrate and go home with clarity on what I really wanted. I wasn't here to be doing this. Whatever *this* was. I wasn't here to be with other women. I could have had many women over the last couple of months, but I wouldn't go there—I knew it was not *why* I was here. And yet, from nowhere, here I was, holding this girl's hands and staring deeply into her soul, knowing that I had found her, knowing that she felt the same—that she had found me.

I have no idea how long we stayed in that space, time stood still. Without a word being exchanged, I placed my hand on her cheek and she gently closed her eyes as a single tear fell. She placed her hand on mine and opened her eyes as she looked into my soul. *Yes. Yes, for now. Yes, for then. Yes, for all the lost time.* Sometimes words do not need to be spoken. I took her hand as we headed for my unit. I was never surer of anything in my life.

∞

Oh, My God, what are you doing? I fought desperately to hold reign over my thoughts. *You don't even know him. He's way older than you. He's probably married. You don't even know his name. Stop. Stop and just go home. Stop!* I took a deep breath to steady myself and my soul sang out in retaliation at the barrage of thoughts desperately trying to drag me from my truth.

'No, you STOP! Shut the fuck up. I am sick of listening to you telling me what to do. Putting fear into me when this time I know. I know what I am doing. I know what I want. I know what is right for me. I just know. I have listened to you for too many years and that is why I'm here. That is why I'm running away from my life, so I can find just a little space and freedom from the constant barrage that you inflict on me. Can't you see that? I'm going crazy constantly listening to you and everyone telling me what I should do and what I should be. I know me. I have always known me. You know what, I fucking miss me. Not the person you tell me I should be, the person I know that I really am. And, you know what, I am going to listen to HER, because I trust her.'

My mind screamed the fear card, *Do you know what is going on here? Can you really trust him? Can you really trust yourself? He may have drugged you?* But not this time! Fuck off fear, my soul disputed.

'You pretend to be my best friend, pretend to keep me safe, pretend to care, but all you really do is hold me back. Hold me back from living my life. Hold me back from being free. Hold me back from being ME. You cannot scare me, because I know with every cell of my body that this is right. I know and I remember and I am listening, and if this is what acting on your knowing feels like, then this is what I want to feel.
This assuredness. This aliveness. This connectedness.
I know him in a way I have never known another. So, don't tell me what I should or shouldn't do. Don't you dare try to keep me small and weak and scared and separate from me.

I KNOW ME! In this moment, I have never been clearer knowing me.'

And I exhaled deeply, laughing and crying as I found my seat within my soul and she beamed as I finally spoke her truth.

∞

God, she is amazing!

Having somehow witnessed the internal battle she had just experienced, I could hardly walk because of the energy surging. She was extraordinary and I craved to feel that energy within me, again. I held her as my mouth found hers. I had never felt anything like that moment, nothing had ever even come close. The energy connecting us was inexplicable, insatiable. My soul had been starved of her for lifetimes. I had found her and I needed more. I had to have more. Nothing else mattered. Not even that I was seventeen years older, as I later discovered. Trust had brought me to this moment, for whatever reason, and trust would take me to the next moment and to the one after that, allowing what will be, to be.

∞

When the fall morning sunlight poked through the curtains of the little room, that she had found herself, she mulled the words, trust and truth. She had trusted herself and she knew that all that had happened was her truth. But there was a nagging curiosity of why. Why had their paths crossed now? Why had she experienced this now? Why now?

Her inner voice guided her. *You do not need to know that answer, just continue to trust what you know and live what you know your truth to be, and all will be okay. All happens for a reason and for the good of all, when you listen and trust and have the courage to live truth.*

She listened and acknowledged this, yet she longed to reach for him again, despite knowing it was not her truth. She ached to know that feeling again. It was not just the feel of a man. It was beyond that. Despite her youth she was not inexperienced in her sexuality. It was something she had embraced from a young age of fifteen with her first boyfriend. She had never shied away, even with others after she and her first boyfriend split. She had never disrespected it either. It was simply a part of who she was; an aspect of herself to be explored and experienced, that she had honoured.

This was different. It was beyond anything she had felt with others. An ecstasy beyond time. An elation of freedom like flying through the sky with nothing holding you back. Knowing you are as bright as the twinkle of a star, as pure as the Divine, and above and beyond everything, that you are without limit—you expand and flow forever. She stifled a giggle, recalling a childlike freedom that overtook her the night before, the freedom to be beyond everything that exists. That first time with him, was gentle and loving, a love so deep and so powerful that she sobbed. A love that cannot exist with a stranger. He was anything but a stranger—he felt like home and for the first time—he took her *home*.

And she turned, grasping at him, needing that again.

She touched his face pleading in desperation. She knew that this time was different. She knew this time not to go there. But this time she told herself otherwise.

When they reconnected, it was as though the picture was complete. Everything was at peace. Everything that was broken was fixed. Everything that was missing was found. Everything that was forgotten was remembered. Everything that was *here* was nothing and everything that was *there* was everything. And they wanted to be there. They wanted to stay, together, as one. His eyes told her, no, we shouldn't.

His groin stirred. He wanted it again. He, too, knew that his whole self, changed when he connected with her—it was epic. He knew enough about energy, through his studies in yoga and meditation, to understand that something had transpired between their souls when their bodies found one another. What they had experienced when their souls reunited, was something that many seek through a lifetime of dedicated spiritual practice, and never find it. And, here they were, having seemingly stumbled across it—a feeling of euphoria, peace and expansion—he too, felt the desire for more. But something deep inside, told him that for them to go there again, would be dangerous.

The whisper within him was silenced when her hand begun trailing its way across his chest and to his lips and then down beneath the covers where she caressed him. As her lips found his, he entered her and they became one. In this space, again they returned home.

With that she soared to places she had never been. She became more than she believed she could. She felt herself expanding and she breathed with it allowing herself to become more. Each breath, she was more. More divine. More powerful. More magnificent. She never wanted it to end.

'Stay with me,' she begged after he released.

He tried to stay with her. But something fractured and he couldn't hold her any longer. And without him, she couldn't stay. She had to come back to the reality of here and she really didn't want to be here. She wanted to stay there.

'I am sorry.'

And while she felt the same deep limitless love for this stranger beside her that she felt the night before, she couldn't help but, now, feel resentment. A resentment for making her come back.

HERE, ME

'My name is Halia. My best friend is *Snow*. And, I want to go home.'

With that, I stuck the needle into my arm and closed my eyes knowing it would only take a moment. Hoping it would last forever, this time. I was not scared. I was not scared when I was a kid. I was free and did whatever I wanted. Nothing really held me back. My parents would laugh that I was like a jippery kitten from the time I woke to the time I slept. Always exploring, always curious and wanting to know more. Always asking adults questions. Which used to really annoy my mum when she was having conversations with her friends and I would interrupt, politely mostly, and ask all sorts of questions about where they were born; where they lived; who was in their family; what they did; if they liked it, or what they were having for dinner. Always curious to know people's stories. And always with my arms out ready to hug people. My mum believed I sensed they needed a hug. I don't recall sensing they needed a hug, I just liked giving big *squeezy* hugs.

I was pulled into this world, lodged so tight within my mother's womb, by all accounts I was not going anywhere. I was twelve days overdue when my mother was induced and then after thirty-four hours of labour, I was delivered by C-Section. It's not that I was in distress or anything, apparently, I just wasn't going anywhere, so they called it and said it was time. I hate that they decided that for me.

My life was wonderful. I had a sister Rosie, two years younger than me. She never really got me. We were just different. I liked to be out running or riding and she preferred to be inside reading. She was born with some sort of heart condition and was often sick, so while she lay around being all sick and stuff and Mum fussed around her, I would just be doing my thing, in my own little world. It was my world. I was free to be me. I just went with it. I liked being by myself. I was never scared by myself. I was always outside. That was my place, outside. I guess I found my way, by taking myself into my own world, where I could just roam with no one else. No one telling me what I should do or say or feel.

I try and take myself there, you know. Back into my weird and wonderful world, and for a while it worked. I could go there and just hang out, feeling free, surrounded by others but all by myself, light and just there, at peace.

Then one day, I couldn't get there anymore. I tried and tried but it was never enough. No matter how much I tried I couldn't get there. That's when I started to try other things to get me there. Firstly, I was mucking around with my friends and I would get such a hit, and it was fun and kept me going. Then I needed it in a way my friends didn't. It wasn't just fun anymore, I needed it. I always made it look like it was fun and just partying, but I knew, and I suppose others knew that it was different for me. It was the only thing that kept me going through the day, knowing that I could go there later. It was like a reward for sticking out another day here. I got to go there.

I needed it.

I desperately needed it.

In the same way as I desperately needed him.

Fuck him. Fuck him for starting this.

When I went to school, it got a little harder to hold on to me. I held on in my own way. Others may have thought I was weird. They called me shy. I wasn't shy. Stupid fuckers. They had no idea who I was. I wasn't shy. I just needed my space. It did get harder and harder to find that extraordinary space and soon I forgot about it. Well, I don't know if I forgot or they just got in. I didn't really have anyone to teach me how to hold onto it and hold onto me. My parents needed easy when my sister got sicker and sicker. Their focus had to be on her. Not that I minded. I don't think I minded. *Did I?* I don't know.

When I was nine, my sister died. I hated her for that because she got to go and I had to stay. I had to stay with Mum and Dad, who somewhere along the way had forgotten about each other, themselves and why they were together. Things were dark at that time. I moved in it and amongst it and maybe it got in, the darkness, maybe the dark got in. I don't know what happened. But my light disappeared as I became ever more invisible in the world. Is that what went wrong with me? I tried hard to get my parents out of the dark. I worked so hard at school, I needed to be the best, so that they had some happiness and they had something good. I was their good and I did all I could to be their good. I became what they needed me to be. That's how I tried to fix them. By being whatever they needed me to be. I was an A-grade student. And I ran. Oh my, could I run—not surprisingly, running worked for me—gave me that hit and made me feel like I could fly. I'd do it over and over and over. Dad really liked me to run, he would coach me. It made him happy. And I got to fly.

Then Dad left. When I was eleven years old he left and I didn't know why. No one bothered telling me why. He just left. Obviously, my good was not enough. My good was not enough to fix him because he left. And when he left, Mum left too, even though she wasn't there anyway. She might as well have gone because she remained so trapped in her own world of pain, struggle and misery that she couldn't even get out of bed most days.

I didn't want to be here, then, so I ran. I ran and ran and ran. The short distant sprinting was not enough after a while. So, I ran longer. The longer I ran the freer I felt. I could almost get myself there again, almost. And I was good at it.

The world started to notice me again. I was smart. I was fast and I was pretty. I was everything the world wanted me to be. I got noticed. In some fucked up way I felt that I was enough again. And yet, I knew that none of this was enough. I knew that none of this was me. I knew that none of this was real. The noise of the outside telling me, I was enough, silenced my inner voice, which told me I was enough already, exactly as I was. But then I couldn't get to it anymore. I couldn't get to that feeling of being enough within me anymore.

Can I leave you now and maybe I'll come back to you one day? But now, it's too hard. It's just way too hard to be here unless I feel like I am enough in how they see me. So, if I'm going to stay here, then I have to be enough for them and that will be enough for me, right?

'I get it,' my inner voice gently acknowledged. 'Know you can come back whenever you need. I am always here for you. The longer you leave it, the harder it becomes to find again, but never stop believing you can. Never forget who you really are, and know you are enough, always and you are loved, always.'

I was fifteen when I made that desperate pact with myself. I knew I was stepping away from me and who I really was. But no one could see me anyway. They could only see me as who they wanted me to be. And, while I longed to be seen, truly seen as me. I still needed to feel enough. I guess I sold out, so that I could feel enough.

I embraced a version of me that, studied, ran, played and I found boys and boys found me. I confidently stepped into that version of myself, selling a picture to the world that I owned my space. I made my choices. I knew what I was doing. I appeared confident and assured in this version of me. Sometimes my friends would laugh at me and say that they were so glad that I stopped being shy and weird and stuff. I'd simply smile as my heart ached. My heart was breaking because I missed me.

Mum seemed to like this version of me and she started to get better and become more engaged with life again. It was what she needed me to be. Either that or her doctors had finally found the right concoction of medications to trick her into thinking that life was okay. I didn't know. Whatever it looked like, it was working and that was the way things were.

Until that day in early fall, when I was seventeen and I woke up in the early hours of the morning and felt like I couldn't breathe. I thought I was dying. I was *not* afraid of that. Oh no, I was not afraid of that. I was petrified of staying here and living like this.

From the pit of my stomach I breathed, hysterically gasping, sobbing, gripping for air with this realisation. I cannot keep doing this. I cannot breathe. I am dying here. I cannot do one day longer like this. I got out of bed, in a trance knowing that I needed to get away. I needed to be alone. I needed the noise to stop. I needed all of this to stop and the only way I knew how to do this was to get away. To be alone again. Outside. Exploring. Moving. Moving fast. Being free.

I took my mother's car and I drove to the mountains. I needed the clean, white purity of the snow around me, within me. Oh, the fucking irony! Time after time I inhaled dirty, filthy snow into me, needing it desperately within me, as desperately as I needed that pure white snow around me that day. That fucking day. That took me there and brought me here with a stomach full of pills and a needle hanging out of my arm.

DESCENDING INTO DARKNESS

On the morning I left him, as I gathered my things we said nothing. Nothing needed to be said because we both knew. As I opened the door to leave, he, the ever so familiar stranger, placed his hand on my shoulder to stop me. Turning me to him, he kissed me gently on the forehead and simply whispered the words, 'Take care.'

I tried to take care when I returned home. I tried to forget about what had happened. It was just too much for me to process. I shut it down and locked it away somewhere deep. Of course, I had to explain why I had taken my mother's car and why I had gone missing. I just lied. No one would understand if I tried to explain why I had gone.

Why I had needed to get away so desperately. Nobody could possibly understand what had happened that night. If I had tried to explain it to my friends they would have dirtied it, tarnished it, destroyed it for me in some way. Even though, I was seething with anger and resentment at him for what happened in the morning. I could not have what happened that night, whatever it was, ruined for me. I needed to hold onto it. Not him, no, I needed to hold onto *that* feeling. How could I possibly share that with anyone? Nobody understood me. I tucked it away deeply within me. My hidden treasure. Little did I know where that choice, a hidden tresure with no key, would lead me.

I settled back into being who I thought I was supposed to be. I just got on with that version I had created of me. Not this weird girl, who runs away to the snow to find her peace. Even though I really liked her.

I didn't go away to college. I stayed in my home town and went to college. I wanted to go. I wanted to get away and I was offered opportunities to study. I felt I should stay here. Close to Mum in case she needed me. And besides, I was safe. My friends were all staying and we could just keep doing what we had been doing, albeit in college rather than school. It wasn't long before I knew that I could not be happy on this path. The darkness was hanging around me and had been niggling for some time. I chose to ignore it, not allowing anyone, especially myself, to see my pain, my struggle, my suffering. I quickly became known as the party-girl. Always keen to go drinking, dancing and playing with boys. I soon discovered, that when I drank it numbed everything and I didn't really feel anything for those few hours. I was the silly, fun, drunk life of the party. The boys loved me, because I was easy. Easy to be with and fun to be around and they knew that. I just let myself go... I was drunk anyway, what did it matter and maybe, just maybe, one of the boys might be able to take me there again. Maybe, maybe not. They were just boys, after all, so I started to seek out men. I looked older and I knew how to play older, so attracting men was not hard for me to do. But they never took me there.

I loved this life. This life that I had created. Simply because I could laugh and dance and feel free from my inner torment for that short period of time. It was fun. I was fun. Everyone loved this fun party-girl. I loved her, because she hid the darkness for me. With time, I knew the darkness would catch up with me and I began to need more and more alcohol, to numb the pain and to get me into that fun persona. I started to smoke pot. Not when I was out, no at that stage I would still just drink. But I found that pot would just sort of hold everything at bay until I could get out drinking. So, I started to smoke before I would go to classes, before I would go to work. But it was fine, because I knew lots of people who smoked pot. I convinced myself it was fine.

And then one day, seemingly from nowhere, the darkness caught me. It was still just me and Mum at home, and this could be quite intense. She still had her own demons, although she was much better than when I was a child. At least she got herself out of bed in the morning.

This morning I decided to skip class as I had the house to myself and I needed space. I felt like I was suffocating, everything became too much. I needed space to breathe. I sat outside in the cool fresh morning air, breathing, enjoying my space, trying to just be, how I used to be able to just be. You know where you could sit and chill and everything would feel okay. I really needed that again. But as I sat there, trying to find that feeling, I felt a bubble expanding within and I didn't know what it was. I was finding it hard to breathe. It was filling me up. I was suffocating. *Go away. Go away. You are not meant to be here*. My mind scrambled trying to regain control. I ran inside, grabbing a bottle of wine and a glass. Telling myself that, I was just giving myself a *me* day, and I could do what I wanted.

As I took the first sip I felt calmer. By the time I had finished my third glass I was back in my comfort. The bubble within me had died down and I could breathe again. Relieved, I enjoyed the numbness as it started to descend upon me. *What the fuck are you doing?* My inner voice was screaming. She didn't get a chance to say much these days. I made sure of that. Between the partying and immersing myself in study, I firmly stayed either in my head or out of it. Either way, there was no room for her. And I liked it that way. I blamed her for taking me to the snow and for him. I should never have listened to her.

Seriously, what are you doing darling girl?

I didn't know. I didn't know what I was doing. I crumbled.

Let it out. Just let it out, darling one.

I couldn't let it out. I didn't want to let it out. I feared it. So, scared that if I started it wouldn't stop.

Just let it out.

I threw first my glass and then the almost emptied bottle of wine. It felt so good. To just throw like that. And the anger came surging through me and I grabbed at everything I could. I threw and smashed and hit and kicked and screamed.

I needed more. I went inside. I hated this place. I hated my mother. I hated her pathetic life. I hated her weakness. I hated her inability to live. I hated my dead fucking sister. I hated her for her pathetic life. I hated her for her weakness. I hated her for her inability to live. I hated her passionately for leaving me here and being there. I wanted to be there. I hated my father. I hated him for leaving me. I hated him for telling me I was not enough by leaving me. I hated him for never saying goodbye. I hated him for never saying hello again, in all these years. As the hatred and anger surged from me, I threw and destroyed everything that I could get my hands on. And it felt so good. So, fucking good.

Then I went to my room and looked into the mirror and I saw a girl looking at me. I didn't know who she was. I hated her. I hated her for who she had become. I hated her for her pathetic life. I hated her for her weakness. I hated her for her inability to live. I looked into her eyes and I saw nothing of the free-spirited girl I once knew. I saw nothing of the girl I had then created her to be. I saw nothing in those eyes. They were dead. I destroyed that nothing that was looking back at me. I smashed the mirror with my bare hands. I loved that pain, as the glass splintered through my palms and fingers. I grabbed at a sliver of the shattered glass and held it in my hand. Squeezing it until the pain shot through me. And the more intense the pain the more I squeezed. The more I wanted it and I squeezed, ripping the glass through my clenched fist. I curled on the ground. Exhausted. Dazed. Blood dripping from my hands.

That is how my mother found me, I don't know how many hours later. I heard her screams as she came into the house. And I felt nothing. I heard her call my name. I felt nothing. I heard her running up the stairs, coming into my room screaming. That hysterical screaming. I felt nothing. My only thought—*fuck you—fuck you all.*

HOPE: A FLICKER OF LIGHT

Once again, I found myself lying in a hospital bed, ten years after my mother found me semi-conscious in a pool of my own blood. In that ten years, it felt like I had done everything I could to get myself into this position again, slowly but surely destroying myself and sabotaging my life.

It was heartbreaking on one level, but there was a different feeling hanging around this time. One that I wasn't familiar with at all. I was here and I was strangely okay with that. I had tried hard not to be and by the looks of things, I got very close. As I lay in a semi-conscious drowsy state I had a bizarre feeling running through me. It felt like excitement. I think I may have found hope somewhere on my trip into the never-never land, because I now knew, deep within that I wanted to be here.

For the last ten years, I had single-handedly worked at removing myself from here, this space and all the pain attached to it. From muting this reality and then attempting to remove myself from it completely. Suddenly, I felt different. I was different. I was absolutely petrified as I had no clue where to begin. But on some level, that didn't matter. I knew that there was a reason for me to be here. I just had to find out what that reason was. There was absolutely no way that I was going to find that mysterious answer if I continued to live my life the way that I had been. I needed change. I was jolted into a massive change.

What jolted me? I didn't see it all happening, I didn't float above my body, like the books and movies say. I have no recollection of anything once that needle met my vein. Maybe it was just a dream, it probably was, but what I saw and felt was beyond real and as I began to come back into consciousness, it clearly remained with me.

I saw myself and then I saw mountains and rivers surrounding me. The greenest and bluest of colours. It was magical. I felt like I was soaring around and through it all —I know that doesn't make sense—but that is how it felt. And then I was stopped, by what I can only describe as a sphere of light, yet it was the most magnificent and compelling golden light you could imagine. And in that space, I knew what I was *supposed to* do. I was supposed to move to the light. Yet, I felt myself being gently turned from the light and in that moment, something changed.

It is not time.

'Yes, I know.'

There is more to do.

'Yes, I know.'

You must return.

'Yes, I know. I know I can come back when my work is done.'

For once, I didn't feel angry and resentful. Finally, I saw and felt it all differently and I knew it was my truth. That feeling of certainty within that I had grappled to find for so long engulfed me. I was certain. I was at peace. A peace contingent on the certainty, that this truth was returning with me. I couldn't navigate my way through life without it.

I ever so gently remembered that it would come to me. It always does. It never left. I just couldn't or wouldn't let myself find it. Yes, my truth was always there. I had always known. I just hadn't wanted to know. I muted the guidance. I muted my inner navigation system. It's no wonder I had been such a train wreck.

In the activation of my inner navigation system, I knew that my part simply involved making sure that I could hear that inner wisdom, that I listened to it and had the courage to act.

I felt overwhelmed at how much work I had to do to find my way back. Back to who I really am. Back to my true self. And as that overwhelm was released by forces outside of me it was replaced by a sense of peace. A deep sense of peace filtered through all aspects of my being. I witnessed the change in my heart rate, my breathing and the tension within my jaw and fists. I saw my physical being respond to the influx of new energy.

It was the start.
I gently returned to my body.
I was peace.
I was awakened.
I was trusting.
I was committed to my truth.
I was ready for change.

Another ten days passed, as I drifted in and out of consciousness not really knowing what was going on around me only what was going on within me. I needed that time from the reality of life; to realign, to prepare, to start the deep healing process before me.

On the tenth day, I broke through my semi-consciousness. The figurative fog lifted.

I was back and I was okay. My eyes scanned the room, absorbing my surrounds. It felt calm and peaceful in here. Someone had been looking after me. I could feel it. Not just physically, but energetically. I knew I was safe and then the door opened, and in walked my father. My father who I had not seen or heard from for almost twenty years.

He smiled, with gentle loving eyes, 'You're back.'
I nodded.

'I'm sorry,' he declared. 'Please forgive me. I love you and I thank you.'

I nodded again as tears ran down my face, 'I remember.' I croaked as my voice was still hoarse from the tubes that had been stuck down my throat, 'You taught me that.'

'I did. And, I have asked this of you for years and telling you tirelessly as you lay here. Praying you would come back.'

'And I have.' I smiled.

'Now come home.'

'Yes. Yes, I will. I will come home.' I was completely assured in my response.

I left the hospital a few days later with my father. Certain that going home with him was where I needed to be. Everyone around me was insistent that this was not where I was meant to be. My mother was furious and full of hatred and resentment towards me for choosing my father. It wasn't a choice I made, there simply was no other choice. Others, do not understand this, because others do not understand me. But they never really have.

I was beyond done with trying to be someone that they can understand, someone that they are comfortable with me being. No more. I have done that little gem for too many years now. That little gem of sabotaging my life experience, just so others understood me. Just so others were happy. It was time for change. Time to seize on that flicker of hope I felt pulsating through my cells and move forward.

It was time.

SNOW THE SEDUCTRESS

As I sat on the sand, I didn't really know what I needed to heal. I didn't know where to begin. It was all sitting in there heavy. But this time, a calm heaviness, not tumultuous. I just didn't know how it was going to shift. But I had faith.

I had been here, with my father for two weeks, the man who abandoned me all those years ago. Yet, somehow, I felt very much at peace. He was intriguing to me. Because he is not the man that I knew as a child. But then I don't think I really had a chance to know him back then. Here, he is now, mystic to me. He has a wise calming presence. Maybe my perception then was not mine, maybe my mother had created it for me.

And so, I sit on this beach. It is his home. He has not

told me much about his life. Respectfully providing me with the space I need and lovingly nurturing me and for the first time in a long time I feel unconditionally loved by someone. Although, part of me is scared. Scared to let him *in*. Scared to be let down and scared to be abandoned again.

I know he is wise and aware of my fears. We have not spoken much. He did say when we flew into Honolulu Airport, 'This is where I came when I left you. This is where I had to come to find my way back. This is my home. May you find yours once again.'

There was something in those words amidst my numbness I felt speak to me. Here I was, this little patch of sand that I had claimed as my own, where I stared for hours at the waves that made this stretch of island famous, rolling into shore. The power and the presence of the waves could have been unbearable, but it was in fact, calming. Perhaps, that was the feeling that surrounded me for the past two weeks, it was quite simply calmness. I hadn't felt this way in a very long time, and I breathed deeply, drawing into every cell within my body. I needed to feel calm now before I went on any further. Maybe, sitting here on this sand, watching the waves and breathing in the calm was the start.

One morning, a few days later, I woke at dawn after a restless night's sleep. I felt irritated and agitated and desperately needed this feeling to go away. I put on my runners and walked downstairs. My father was sitting at the kitchen bench, watching the sunrise.

'Running won't make it go away. You've run for too long now. Go sit on the beach and allow it.' He gently but firmly guided me.

I wanted to tell him to, 'fuck off'. I was sick of everyone telling me what they thought was best for me to do. But I didn't have it in me. I was exhausted fighting everyone, fighting life. I knew he was right. I knew if I started running again it would all go away for a while, and then the running would not be enough to keep it at bay and then I would need more and more and more, and there was never enough to keep it from anonymously haunting me.

Standing there I knew, it was never going to leave me until I was enough.

It was time to stop running. I returned to the beach. The stillness of the previous weeks prepared me for the first layer to reveal itself, to present itself to be explored, experienced, grieved, forgiven, healed. I knew as I peeled that first layer away, that it would make room for new energy to fill that void. And what filled that void, what needed to fill that void would not always be pretty and would not always be easy to face. But sitting there, ready to open myself to my darkness and pain, I made a commitment to myself that I would continue peeling away the layers of darkness engulfing my soul in whatever way I had to, until I reached the core.

Until, I found me again. I knew she was in there and I remembered I loved her. That was my motivation. To stand with, and as her, again.

That first layer was Christopher. He loved me so much in the beginning. He loved me in a way I could never love him. I convinced myself that I was not enough for him and his world, and yet the reality was, he was never enough for me. He never could be.

I didn't know this, then. Because my secret lover was so deeply hidden within me. And on some level, I had loved him. He saved me from me at a time when life was heading in a downward direction. He saw beyond the person I had created myself to be and believed I was worth fighting for. Despite what his family and friends thought. Despite what his mother thought.

I was young, straight out of law school and in my first professional role, as a lawyer in a large firm. Despite my destructive nature and the turbulence of my life, I was smart. I was street smart and intellectually smart and both worked in my favour during my time studying for my law degree. And, once finished I finally moved away. New York City was where I was determined to start a new life.

I had a great job with a sought-after company. I was living in a tiny gorgeous apartment. I made friends. I met men. I had a fabulous social life. And yet, it wasn't enough. I couldn't find that feeling. I thought by changing my life—by moving away, by playing grown-ups with a real job where no one knew my story—that I could forget the emptiness. And, find enough joy in all of that, to become satisfied in this world. But it didn't work out that way.

The novelty wore off quickly. Too quickly. I continued the façade of having it *all* while I was at work. Outside of work, I searched. More running and cross training, more men, more alcohol and more marijuana. The same old story. Then I found it for the first time. I would never forget that first time. I had finally found what I had been searching for. As I sniffed, and let-it-dance-in-my-nostrils. I felt it coming, slowly at first and then it became more intense moving up and outside of my body, and then it throbbed through me. I expanded, each pulsation expanded me further, beyond what I thought was possible. And I beckoned it, I did not resist. This was *it*. I laughed a crazy woman kind of laugh knowing I had finally found it. I had finally fucking found it again. I forgot about finding anything and I simply went there and I danced in that space, floated in that space; I flew in that space, and I allowed myself to be whatever I wanted to be. There were no rules only freedom, peace, ecstasy. So, I gifted myself with more. Every night I pleasured myself with more. I was surrounded by people who loved this up and coming lawyer by day, turn party-girl by night. They wanted to be around me. Because I could take people there, with me.

I saw through them. They didn't love me. They loved who they needed me to be. They meant nothing to me. None of them. They were merely a façade, a party posse, that enabled me to dance my dance with my best friend, *Snow*. And I did. I danced and played with her every night for almost a year. And yet, nobody cared. I did my work, I got results, got promoted and made more money and then I indulged in more Snow. I needed a lot more now than I did in the beginning. It was like she was holding back on me. She wouldn't quite get me there, she teased me, enticing me to take a little more; a little more, a little more. And each time that little more would just get me there. Until it didn't. It soon became just a little in the morning to get me going. How long could one function on only a couple of hours' sleep? A little in the morning wouldn't hurt I told myself. Breaking my own promise that I would never take it to work. My next broken promise was if it started to affect my work, then I would stop. Until now it hadn't, but now, I couldn't stop and I wasn't the one making the decisions any more. She was, my best friend Snow.

Then one morning, a few weeks into my new routine just after our mid-morning catch up in the toilet cubicle I found my manager sitting in my office. Waiting for me. I took a deep breath as I walked in feeling like a naughty school girl but determined to hold my space.

He looked me up and down in disgust and said, 'You've got a problem and I really don't give a damn what you do with your life. Mess it up all you like, just don't mess it up here, because it's not just your reputation on the line. Get yourself some fucking help or get yourself a new job.'

What he said didn't bother me too much, I was impervious to the viciousness of his attack. My only concern was for my job. If I lost my job I'd have no money and I couldn't, well, I just couldn't live in the way I had accustomed myself to living. No money equals no Snow. Well, that was not an option. I had to get it together to be able to keep my job. He was right. I needed help.

The Universe delivered help. Christopher. My future husband. The one who would save me and break me again.

MY SHINING
ARMOURED ONE

Christopher leant against the doorframe to my office, 'Want to grab a coffee, you look like you need one.'

A coffee was the last thing I needed. I was still high. I knew I needed something so I grabbed on. Despite never having had much to do with him, I knew Christopher was a nice guy. We worked in a big company and even though we worked in the same area, and would exchange pleasantries it never extended beyond that. To be honest, my relationship with most people I worked with was very much on a superficial level. I went there, did my work and would immerse myself in my other world. The world where I could play with Snow and be me.

I kept everyone at arms distance. I didn't allow myself to get close. Sure, I had friends and short term boyfriends, but they never got close. They were just there to fill a space.

Now, here was this guy, standing in my doorway offering me a way to get out of this space. A space I was suffocating in, so even if it was just twenty minutes, it would do. I needed to digest what my manager had just spat at me.

Christopher ordered a coffee. I ordered a green tea.

As the waitress walked away, I looked up to see this smirk on his face, 'Green tea?' With one eyebrow raised. 'How very clean of you.'

I laughed. What else could I do? Claim I was some sort of health freak. It was obvious that everyone knew about my secret, or not so secret life.

'Don't mind Carson, he's just a prick who only cares about himself and how he looks to the partners. You know this world. Look after number one. Get there faster and do whatever it takes to get there.'

'I know. I know. I'm just a potential road bump on his way to becoming a partner,' I laughed. 'I know how to play the game. Bad move on my part.'

'Well that's pretty obvious.'

I looked at him kind of confused and somewhat defensive, 'What do you mean?'

'You don't get it at all, do you?'

'What?'

Starting to feel somewhat irritated by him and his

apparent condescending manner.

'You. Everyone has been watching you in awe for the last two years. You came in here, just got on and did your thing and look where you are.'

'Where I am?'

I am sitting here with a guy I barely know who is talking shit. Drinking fucking green tea. Which I hate by the way. Trying to hold onto my high for as long as I can despite feeling it wane. Which I hate by the way.

'What are you talking about?' I laughed at the absurdity of the situation I had found myself in.

'You're some sort of enigma. You just arrived in this office and sent every guy in the place into a spin and put every girl in the place on edge. You put your head down and did your thing completely oblivious to the impact you were having on the people around you.'

Because, I don't give a fuck about the people around me. I somewhat politely refrained from saying.

'I know you don't care about anyone around you and that is what makes you such an enigma. You come, do your thing, disappear into the night, return looking like you've stepped out of *Vogue*, do your thing again, get promoted and promoted and promoted again. You get the great clients and everyone is saying, 'who is she?''

I was slightly bemused and intrigued by this insight into how I was perceived.

'But you've screwed up,' he stated bluntly. 'Everyone noticed how suddenly you weren't looking so glamourous and how you were off your game in general.'

I was no longer bemused. I was angry and humiliated. Pissed off that they all just sat back watching and waiting for me to trip up.

'So, everyone has a bad day here and there,' I pitifully attempted to defend myself.

'Yes, but you don't. See that's the difference. When you started to drop-the-ball it was obvious something was going on.'

I wasn't sure I needed this truth after the morning. I just wanted to get out of the office without a lecture. I felt sad as well. Not that I would ever show that. My work colleagues had sat back watching me set myself up for a fall and not reached out to help. I knew that was of my own doing. I wouldn't have let them in even if they had tried.

'I wanted to help you sooner,' Christopher gently said as if reading my mind. 'Call me superficial but when I noticed your hair lose its shine and your face begin to pallor I wanted to say something. But who was I to say anything? And then, it seemed like you got back on track.'

I'd got myself back on track by bringing my friend Snow, to work. The pretty shiny me got herself together and plastered on that façade, that apparently, everybody loved to see, or maybe didn't love to see.

'You seemed back on your game and looking the part. But the trips to the toilet every morning around the same time were a dead give-away. That's when they all started talking. And once it starts going around like that it's not long before the partners hear about it. You know that.'

Of course, I knew that. What he didn't realise was I didn't have a choice. I couldn't look at him. This stranger, Christopher, who was on the one hand lecturing me and on the other seemed to care about me more than anyone had in a long time. I felt so sad. Desperately sad as a tear fell onto the table followed by another and another.

He slid a napkin across the table, 'It'll be okay.'

I looked up. Completely terrified at what lay ahead for me.

'I don't know if it will?'

I wiped my eyes and looked at this man before me with gratitude. I went back to work intent on finishing the day so I could go out and escape these thoughts and feelings later. Snow would make it better. I didn't know what else to do. But it seemed Christopher did.

The next morning, just as I hit that point of needing to head into the bathroom and knowing that I was risking everything, he appeared at my office door.

'Coffee?'

Feeling anxious but grateful I took a deep breath, 'Sure.'

We stood in the lift and feeling very humble I looked at him and thanked him for his support. He just smiled.

'I need this job you know. You have no idea how much these shoes cost,' I laughed pointing to my *Jimmy Choo's*. 'And everything else,' I shamefully admitted, 'I can't afford to lose this job not where I am at now.'

'It'll be okay,' he gently squeezed my shoulder

reassuring me that it would in fact, be okay.

I suppose that was where it started. He cared. And it felt nice to be cared for. Little by little I let him in. It was okay.

THE BAND-AID
APPROACH

Our daily coffee breaks, soon became late dinners after work. Just one night a week to begin with. Dinners where we would sit and talk for hours, leaving no time to play with Snow. I didn't need her on these nights. Being with Christopher was enough.

And then the dinners went from one night a week, to two and three nights. To be honest, during this time, there was nothing physical between us. It felt like I finally had someone who had my back. I had found a big brother of sorts. And I liked how that felt.

With my partying significantly reduced and relegated to weekends alone, my work got back on track, my job felt secure again, my health improved, I started running again and the fog seemed to lift. That fog that had been hanging so heavily for years, finally faded away.

When the fog faded, I saw what had been in front of me for the last six months. An amazing man, who had put his own job on the line for me. He had cared for me and believed in the girl he saw behind the façade. I realised he would do anything for me and he completely and utterly adored me.

I got out of my own way and I found love.

It was intense, beautiful, blissful. We were incredibly happy. I was incredibly happy. It was magic. I could not remember the last time I felt true happiness. Well I could, but it was tucked away deep within me, locked in the treasure chest. I was too scared to allow myself that memory, because I knew that was what I truly wanted.

But this, well this was enough. This was more than enough, for me.

Within months we had moved in together. We continued to work together. Both forging ahead in our careers. We trained together every morning. We ran together on weekends. We ate brunch at trendy cafes on Sunday mornings. It was perfect. We were perfect. Almost too good to be true. We loved each other. Until his mother got involved.

I hate that woman. I don't feel anger or anything else towards her just a steely dark hatred. It wasn't like that to begin with. In the beginning, I tried to see through her Upper East Side snobbery. I tried to see her for the person she was beneath the disguise. I tried to allow her to like me. I tried to be more like her precious daughter-in-law, who could do no wrong. I tried to be what she needed me to be. I tried to ignore her blatant degrading comments about me. I tried desperately to pretend not to notice that Christopher didn't defend me. Fortunately, we were so busy with our life, that we didn't have to spend a lot of time with her, not in the first whirlwind year that we were together anyway. So, she wasn't really an issue. At least she was an issue that could be ignored. A simmering wound hidden by a band-aid slapped on to make it go away. The day we announced our engagement, was the day the band-aid was brutally ripped off.

'Halia, please leave the room, darling,' I was politely ordered, after Christopher told his mother that we planned on marrying. She did everything so politely.

I left the room, as *politely* ordered, but stood just outside the door, close enough to hear her *politely* begging her son.

'Oh, but you barely know her and you are so young. What is the rush? There is plenty of time. You might find someone that you like more, darling. It is very quick.' She pushed on. 'What if you find out that you don't really like her? Of course, I can see the attraction, darling. She is stunning, but sweetheart, that doesn't last forever. What if under that pretty little face and those long legs there's not much else there and you find out she's not the one. You know she's not our kind. I would prefer you waited. Do you really know her? You never know what you could be getting. She could just be after the money, darling.'

I stood there completely mortified and stupefied that this woman had the nerve to speak so condescendingly and derogatorily to her son about me. I was beyond horrified that Christopher had not spoken up to defend me. I couldn't hold back any longer.

'I am not after his, or your money,' I stood firmly in the doorway. 'I am quite able to support myself, as I always have and as I still do. Christopher knows all there is to know about me. Warts and all. And, guess what. He has still chosen me. So, there must be something worth loving beyond this pretty little face and these long legs. I'm leaving now. Have a lovely evening.'

I left alone and on my way home, I found a *new* band-aid. One that would be sure to make this simmering problem disappear, or at least block it out so that it didn't bother me so much. That band-aid not surprisingly was my trusted friend, Snow. But this time, I convinced myself, I was not using her to try and find that elusive place, as I thought I had found something along those lines in my life with Christopher. And I needed to hold onto that. But I knew my future mother-in-law wasn't planning on going anywhere and I knew I would need help and I would do whatever it took to hold onto this life with Christopher. This time Snow was just helping to take the edge off my feelings—my anger, resentment, bitterness, inadequacy, fear, vulnerability—all emotions that were going to get in the way and cause us problems.

When Christopher returned home later that evening,

the edge had been taken off my altercation with his mother and my resentment towards him and his apparent lack of support was beautifully numbed. Perfectly suppressed.

As the mood seemed much lighter than he anticipated, he chose not to bring up the issues with his mother and he also chose not to question why I was in a much better mood than he expected. On some level, I suspect he knew that my old friend may have popped in and paid me a visit for the afternoon, but in a way, I don't think he wanted to know. It was easier not too, or so it seemed.

This was the beginning of a new game for us. A game that served us well for a couple of years. A game that got me through our wedding day, when I was dealing with the absence of my father and Rosie, the presence of my mother and my silently brewing rage at my soon to be mother-in-law, who let her true feelings towards me and my marriage to her son be expressed privately. Despite the public declarations that I was the most amazing young woman and it was the happiest day of her life.

A game that got Christopher and I through many social engagements when my feelings of inadequacy in the world he had grown up in could have made for a very uncomfortable night for both of us.

A game that we pretended wasn't at play.

A game that well and truly was at play.

A game called: Let's stick our head in the sand and pretend there's not a problem.

We played the game and we played it beautifully.

I don't know if Christopher knew there was a third party in our marriage. I don't know if he knew I was playing around with Snow again. If he did know, he either chose not to care or he chose not to address it because it was just easier playing the game. When I played with Snow, then I was enough for him. I was enough for his mother. I was enough for his friends. I ticked all their fucking boxes. I felt I was enough and I suppose everything was well when everyone was happy. I convinced myself that this was the way that it had to be because I could not lose Christopher or this life that I had created. To the outside world, Christopher and I had it all. A beautiful marriage, successful careers, a lavish home, an abundance of money, fabulous holidays and a wonderful social life. We ticked the fucking boxes.

Snow saved my marriage, because with Snow, I was what Christopher needed me to be. Snow also ruthlessly stole my soul. I was nothing. I was empty. I was dying inside.

One day, after a bitter argument with Christopher over his mother and the toxic hold she had on him, I saw the game for what it was. I saw that I had been playing along to this fucking pretence as well. I had somehow convinced myself because I was doing it my way, with Snow, without anyone knowing, that I was somehow different to the rest of them and I wasn't part of the game. The great big façade!

And then the ugly truth hit me and I couldn't hide. I was as much a part of this game as anyone else. I was no better than anyone else, in fact, I was probably worse than all of them. All of them that I had grown to despise because of their weaknesses. I decided that I didn't want to be here anymore living my life as a lie. One huge big lie. One in which I was not enough for Christopher and one that was not enough for me. A life that was a fucking failure!

Life was a joke. And I was a joke to think I could ever find that elusive feeling that I had been chasing for years, here in this fucking life.

I was done with it here. I wanted to be there now. I desperately wanted it again. Snow couldn't take me there anymore, the truth was she never really could—and now she couldn't even get close—she had run her course. She abandoned me when I needed her most. Just like everyone else. She was nothing more than the band-aid over the fucking reality I was living. The pathetic life I had created and it was empty and dark and I was done.

And, with a stomach full of pills and a needle in my arm, I was determined I wasn't coming back.

SIMMERING VOLCANOS
EVENTUALLY ERUPT

Some days sitting on the beach in Hawaii, I would wonder what I was doing there. Dad was Hawaiian, but I never had more of a connection than that. I suppose because he didn't seem to have much of a connection to Hawaii either. And yet, as I sit on the beach, listening to the waves roll in, I am connected to this place.

When Dad appeared at the hospital and asked me to 'come home', I knew what he meant. I had no doubt that this was where I needed to be. It is the closest thing to home that I have ever experienced. I feel safe and nurtured and just able to flow with the day.

I suppose stepping out of New York City and the hectic

corporate world and a social life intimately entwined with that corporate life, will do that. For they are polar-opposites in terms of energy and flow. But this is where I needed to come. Perhaps the whole polar-opposite was what was needed. I mean things were extreme.

I know no one can really understand why I am here. I know they think I am just running away and having a holiday. A sabbatical or some rehab. Again, maybe it is both packaged differently. But this is not a little holiday. I wasn't going back, not to New York City and my old life, my old ways. That story was over. I'd stay here until I healed. Until it was time to move on. I choose not to think about the future. Only this moment. Focusing on the sound of the waves and getting back in tune with the flow of *me*.

I adored Dad when I was a kid. But then he left and I never was told why and I never understood. Now, there is this man in my life, who I know is my father but I do not know who he is. He gives me space, but is ever so gently guiding me along whatever it is I am doing here.

He asked for my forgiveness in the hospital. And I forgave him. Yet, I still wonder how I could forgive him after he had abandoned me. He suddenly just turned up from nowhere seeking my forgiveness. Yet I offered it to him, without hesitation, because after all I had been through, I simply needed peace in my life and forgiving him, seemed like the first step to that peace. If I had let the drama in, the old story and said I couldn't forgive him for what he did to me, my mother, to my life—then

I would still be in there—I was tired of that life. It was weighing me down. It was killing me. It almost did kill me. I could see in his amazing turquoise blue eyes, as he asked for my forgiveness, that he needed it. He was still in pain and he needed my forgiveness to ease that pain. Why should he be in pain anymore? It was done.

In forgiving him, I freed myself from that story and I freed him, well, so I thought. The lightness, the gentle ease permeating from him, that I felt when we first returned to Hawaii, started to fade after a few weeks. I thought it may have been because of me. Because I was still very heavy myself. I was carrying so much grief, anger, frustration and despair. I thought that perhaps my negativity was rubbing off on him. And yet, he moved through his days and continued his work as before, but there was something there. I just couldn't figure out what.

A few days, after I had my first big breakthrough on the beach, where I had released all my stuff over Christopher, I decided to ask my father if he was okay. After all, I was feeling much better. I was lighter, free, calm and at peace, secondary to shedding my first layer of emotional baggage.

Slightly oblivious of course, that once that first layer goes, it can only be days or weeks before the next layer starts fermenting and letting you know that it is ready to go, too. I didn't realise that was how it worked when I first began my healing. I thought shifting the painful memories around my life with Christopher was all I needed to do, that I was pretty much done, as it had made such a huge difference to me. So, *naïve*. It was just the beginning. That wonderful feeling—of being light, when you haven't truly—and I mean truly (no chemicals added), felt it for so long, you are almost lulled into a false sense of peace.

This was the space I was in and without the heaviness weighing me down, I was able to notice my father and I could sense his sorrow within. He had given me time and was very respectful of my privacy, not asking me any questions. We had, in those first couple of weeks, established the unspoken way of being together. He looked after me and I allowed him to take care of me.

However, this morning, as we sat in companionable silence on the deck, listening to the distant waves rolling in, with the sun shining down upon us and the heat of late spring settling in for the day, I felt compelled to break our unspoken rule.

I asked him, 'Are you okay, Dad?'

'Of course, sweetheart. I am better than I have ever been. I have you here with me and I know you are going to be okay. That makes me okay,' he gently squeezed my arm and then looked back out into the distance with that sadness still present in his eyes.

Just leave it, I thought. *It's not your right to go imposing yourself on him and you don't need his stuff, you've enough of your own.* My heart ached a little and I simply had to reach out to him.

'Dad, you seem sad,' I tried to be so gentle. He didn't look at me. 'Is it me? Am I making you sad by being here?'

'Ah,' he smiled as he turned to me, with tears in his eyes. 'You being here, has brought me more happiness than I have ever experienced in my life. What you have done for me in forgiving me for the unforgivable I will never forget. You freed me from a weight so heavy that I have carried all these years.'

'Then why are you sad?'

'Because the happiness I feel now, has highlighted how much I have missed. All that I missed in sharing your life. In how your life may have been different, less painful, if I had not left you. I am feeling this sadness. And, that is okay because I have to feel it, really feel it, really know it, really experience it. Then I will figure out how to release it, and I will.'

I nodded. Not really understanding fully.

'You know how you are feeling today with that lightness and calm? Don't think I haven't noticed the change in you. I am so happy for you and so proud of you for doing your work. You are feeling this because you have let go of so much stuff. And when we get rid of our emotional baggage. It creates space. Space that is then filled with something new. Sometimes though, the new, is not always a wonderful feeling, like sadness. But that is okay. It is perfect. It has come because it is what needs to fill the space for now. Because I need to heal my deep sadness now. And you will learn that if it is not something that you desire to feel, once you have learnt all you need to learn from it, you will release it. And the cycle continues. It is like you with your shoes. Seriously, how many pairs of shoes does a girl need?'

'You haven't even seen a quarter of them.'

My father had already noticed my love affair with shoes. I had Christopher pack me some things, but most of my stuff had been put in storage. Rightly or wrongly, he had packed me about ten pairs of shoes, even though I had only worn thongs and runners since I had been here.

'Yes, like your shoes. You will get rid of some, I hope, to make space, right?' He teased.

'Yes occasionally. I get your point. If I get rid of some of my dearly beloved shoes, then I can make space for some more. Perfect scenario!'

'Yes, but sometimes the new shoes you buy, well they aren't quite the right fit, they don't feel right. You might hang onto them for a while, but eventually, when the time is right, you will get rid of them to make more room for when the right ones come along. The ones that fit just right, that make you feel amazing, fit perfectly with all the others in the wardrobe—and, completely compliment who you are—these ones, you will hold onto forever and never let anyone take them from you.'

I got it and wondered what was to come next for me.

'I will let go of this sadness soon. I just feel I need to sit with it a while longer. I will know when the time is right. When that time is right, I will be ready to forgive myself for leaving you.'

'I have forgiven you already, Dad, in the hospital remember?' I asked confused.

'And I thank you again. I needed it. I needed that

for a long time, for many years. Thank you for gifting me your forgiveness. That forgiveness has created space for the sadness and that is okay. I now need to forgive myself. It is very different to the forgiveness of others. In many ways, it is more powerful. I feel in some ways I have been punishing myself all these years, in subtle ways for having left you when I did. But soon, it will be the time, time when I find it within myself to stop the punishment and forgive. It will be interesting what that will allow into my life.'

We sat in silence. I was mulling on his words. Wondering about him, and the life that he had created here when he left and how he had become so wise about these things. This was not the man I knew as a child. I suppose I am not the person he knew as a child either. The difference being, he had changed for the better. I had not. Was this his fault? I didn't know. I really couldn't recall, what impact him leaving had on me. One day he was just gone. I was angry. I did hate him, for a while, and then it was just the way it was. I felt nothing. I still didn't understand why Dad left though and I felt a slither of something I didn't like the feel of bubbling in my stomach.

Go away. Go away, I don't want to feel this. I want to just be okay with everything. Well, that is what I tried to tell myself. I wanted it to all be shiny and okay again. *Don't bubble. Don't fill me with that rage. I hate that feeling. Just fuck off!* I wormed around on my seat, starting to feel irritated. I think I needed to go for a run or something.

Dad turned to look at me, with his eyes questioning me.

'What?' I snapped.

'Are you okay?'

'Yes, I'm fine.' I snapped again.

'It's alright to feel it. You must in fact.'

'I don't want to feel it. Don't you understand that. I don't want to feel this. I am so fucking over it. I don't want it there,' I argued, sobbing.

'Then let it out. Don't keep stuffing it away. Masking it up. Making yourself feel better with other stuff,' he gently, yet firmly told me.

I tried to take a few deep breaths to calm down, but it was almost like this volcano within had started to erupt and I couldn't contain it, no matter how many deep breaths I took. Each breath seemed to fuel it more. I erupted. I turned to him, full of indignant rage, impossible to contain.

'How did you get so fucking wise? It's easy to sit there and preach about what I should do to heal. When you were the one who broke me. You all were. I hate you. I hate you all. You and Mum and Rosie. You all left me and I'm so pissed off with you all. So, fucking pissed off. I have felt like this forever and it has taken everything I am not to be this person. To not be this angry person. I don't want to be this fucking angry person. You know, I let it out once. I destroyed the house. Mum found me and I had trashed the house and myself. I was so angry with the world and I cut myself and destroyed everything that reminded me of you and her and Rosie and it felt so good to cut myself. To hurt myself so I could really feel the pain. The pain that I had ignored since you left me. No one was there to tell me why. Mum never told me why. You, you never fucking told me why. You just left me. I thought you loved me,' I spat indignantly. 'Mum left me years before when Rosie got sick. I didn't exist for her. Maybe I never really existed for her? And then Rosie left me. And then you left me and *he* left me. He left me alone, by myself.' I paused in my rage, confused as to where that had come from. I ignored it. Tucked it away again, back in the treasure chest where it could not hurt me.

I turned on my dad again. It was him I was angry with. It was him I was angry with, no one else.

'Why did you leave me?' I demanded still raging. Tears of bitterness and confusion, streaming down my face.

My father stood and placed his hand on my shoulder.

'Come, let's go inside and make another tea and I will tell you. I will tell you everything. You can then choose whether you want to truly forgive me or not.'

I followed him, my rage calmed somewhat by his gentleness and his vulnerability. I knew he didn't leave me to hurt me. Not purposely and I knew I had already forgiven him. I needed to know his story.

DAD'S STORY

'We were really happy, your mother and me. We were young lovers, who met while she was here on holidays with her friends. She was eighteen. I was twenty-one and we were inseparable while she was here. When she left, I missed her so much I followed her home. Leaving all my family, friends and all that I knew. At the time, none of that mattered. I loved her so much. We were happy.

We settled into life. I got my own place and found a job and she was still living with her folks and at college. It was nice and simple. We sort of got to know one another properly.

Then your mother fell pregnant with you. And being religious, her family made us marry. There was never a question of not having you. But we were young and marriage was certainly not on the cards for either of us.

We married and she moved into my little place and we were happy and excited about you. I suppose we were quite naïve playing happy little families and didn't really know what we were in for. I picked up a second job, to try and save for our own house while your mother was pregnant with you and still studying.

I think this started the pattern. I worked a lot and she was alone a lot. She didn't seem to mind when she was studying and had a bit of a social life with her friends. But once you were born, that all changed. She was nineteen, with a baby and a husband who worked a lot. I don't think her family ever forgave her for the shame of getting pregnant before she was married. She didn't get much support from them. She struggled and I didn't know how to help her. I wasn't there for her in the way I should have been. I didn't know any different. I was the man. I wanted to provide for my little family. It was in my blood, my DNA, that as the man, I provided. And I did.

The doctor must have been given her some anti-depressants or something. I should have known, but I didn't. I did care, but didn't know how. And then we bought our house and your mum seemed a little happier, with the house and the tablets. She dutifully kept house and looked after you and she took so much pride in you, her home and her little family. We were happy. In a different way to before. But the happiness was still there. It really was.

She then fell pregnant with Rosie. We were both so

excited. And yes, probably both a little overwhelmed at the idea of having another child but delighted for you having a brother or sister. When she arrived, you doted on her like a mini-mumma. You were like two peas in a pod, only eighteen months apart. Rosie was not an easy baby, she would cry all night and your mother would be up with her, and then up all day with you. I was still working two jobs, sixteen hours a day and I needed sleep. I should have helped her more. Things got quite bad.

The doctors seemed to get things under control with the medications and she was able to cope a bit better. But she, well, she wasn't the same person, she was sort of empty inside when she took the medication. But we didn't know what else to do. I wasn't there for her. Not in the way I should have been.

Fortunately, life settled down a little after those first few years. I got promoted, so I didn't need to work two jobs. Your mother went back to college to study when you girls went to school. Your mother got well again, and could finally stop the medication. And she came back to herself. Those years were so good. They really were. Years of simple happy family times. I treasure them so much. That is when we were all happy.

Then Rosie got sick. She was always more fragile than you. You were a strong robust, sporty, fiery, curious, crazy kid. While Rosie was very gentle, calm, and yeah, I suppose a little fragile in many respects. She was a perfect balance for you and even though you were different, you meshed together perfectly. Everything changed when

Rosie got sick.

I couldn't handle any of it. I had to keep working because the medical bills were massive. Your mother was there for Rosie. She was her rock. She was amazing. But inside she was dying herself. Each day just a little more. She knew quite quickly that she needed to get back on her medications to help her through because Rosie needed her and she was able to be there for Rosie, but she had nothing else left. Nothing left for you. I wasn't there for you either.

Oh, my darling girl. I'm so sorry. When Rosie went. When our beautiful angel left us, things only got much worse. Your mother and I had grown apart, living such separate lives and we were both stuck in our own pain, our own grief. We did not know how to support each other. Your mother was numb to the world and despite her medication, dropped deeper and deeper into her depression. Trapped in there. You were my joy.' Dad paused. He hung his head, a tear dropping onto the table beneath him.

I felt so sad, as I saw the grief wash over my father.

Grief for the loss of the life that he had created.

'My time with you, Halia, was my only joy. I looked after you. And you kept me alive. But then I had to start working another job again, as the medical bills meant we almost lost our home. And that is what our life became for two years. Me working. Your mother in bed. And you, my little lost girl, just floated in there, amongst the emptiness, the sadness and despair. The only light in my life.'

But I wasn't enough. I wanted desperately to scream, *I wasn't enough because you still left me. I was not enough light for you!* My eyes, must have said it all, because he continued.

'Oh, my darling, if only you knew. I wouldn't have lasted as long as I did, if it was not for you. But, I knew I had to leave, because I was dead and my life was spiralling out of control. Your mother was cold, distant and hopeless—no matter what I did to try and help her—she did not want to come out of her darkness. I now understand that she believed on some level, that if she stayed in there, she would be closer to Rosie. I begged her to get more help because you needed her. I needed her back—the woman I had fallen in love with—I missed her.

But she would just blankly say, 'If I come back, then I will leave Rosie and I cannot do that, it is not fair on her'. I think she felt that it would be some sort of insult or injustice to Rosie, if she started living again. I understood that on some level. But there was you. And you deserved your mother too.'

And my father. I deserved my father too. But you left me too. You left me with her. I wanted to yell all of this, but it remained stuck, burning in my throat.

'I was becoming someone I did not like. I started to

drink. And I am ashamed to say, there were other women. They just filled a void, it was never anything serious. Something to replace the numbness, the emptiness. But as you know, it is never enough and so you go looking for something else and that's not enough either. I had lost myself and I was dying a little more each day living that way. I was destroying myself. And I couldn't see a way back, not while I was still there. That is why I had to go. I had to go and find me again and I couldn't do it there. I had to come home. Here, to my family, to the ways that I knew as a child. To the traditional ways. It came to me one night, that I had to leave. And I knew it to be true and I couldn't ignore it. I tried to ignore it, because of you. How could I leave you there?'

The tears fell down my face as I sobbed, 'Then why did you leave me there?'

'Oh, my darling. I am so sorry. I have been so sorry every day of the last nineteen years. You have been with me every one of those days. I had to make a choice and I chose me. I chose me because I couldn't see how I could ever find my way back if I stayed. It was a selfish choice. But it was the choice I knew to be true for me. I did want to take you. I even spoke to a friend who was a lawyer and he said it would never happen. She would never let me take you from her. She had already lost one daughter and she would never let me take another daughter from her.'

'Bull shit,' I let it out. 'I might as well have been dead to her anyway. She took no notice of me. You knew that and you still left me with her. You knew that, and you still left me.'

'Halia, I vowed every day, that I would make it worth leaving you. I sacrificed you for me. I had to make that worth it. I found out how to heal me and I did my work every day. I was relentless with it. I left no stone unturned, as each new layer of anger, grief, fury, sorrow, resentment, sadness, rage and heart-break surfaced, I would do my work around it, diligently. It was all I allowed in my life, for many years after I returned home here. Here was the only place where I could do this work. Where I could heal. I did nothing but go to work and do my healing work. I discovered many amazing practices. I'd do yoga and meditation daily, religiously! I carried so much shame and guilt and remorse for leaving you and it was these emotions that were driving my almost fervent addiction to this work, my pursuit of finding *me* again. Yet, I couldn't get there, until one day I realised my behaviour was not dissimilar to your mother in relation to Rosie. I was not allowing anything or anyone else into my life, out of guilt for leaving you. In a way I was punishing myself, just as your mother was for Rosie leaving.

If I stepped fully into *me* and my life then I really would leave you behind, and I couldn't do that. I was holding onto you and denying myself happiness because of it. I knew that to fully heal, and come back to me and embrace my life, I needed you to forgive me. I couldn't get that from you then, so I committed myself to making it worthwhile. Making the sacrifice and the pain I caused you count.

That is when I began my work with the children. The children who have no one else really looking out for them. I began my programs with the kids and it made a difference, I could see it. In their lives and it made the hugest difference to me. I suppose, that pacified, in a way, the underlying guilt and shame I carried. I know the irony of the situation. That I was compelled to help these kids who had no one to help them and guide them through their troubles, to compensate for not being there to help and guide you. I am so sorry. I know how painful that must be for you.

Then Theresa came into my life. She was a little older than me. She started volunteering on the program and it was like a piece of my soul was returned to me when she came into my life. She was an angel sent to me, I have no doubt, and she brought me back out, back out into life and into living fully. We were blessed. And the great irony of my life, was just when I truly re-emerged into my life and allowed myself to live again, she was taken from me. So quickly. The cancer took over her so quickly. And in a matter of weeks she was gone.

But what she taught me in the few years that I had with her, and especially in those last few weeks before she passed, was so incredible. So, powerful. She opened me more and more to life and the real meaning of life. And being with her when she passed was the greatest gift.

I felt her leave, and then I felt her with me again, just in a different way. I feel her with me all the time. I feel her here now. And, it doesn't make me sad, it makes me happy, because I know she would be so happy that you are here with me and I am finally telling you my story.

She encouraged me to talk about you, in a way I had never been able to talk to anyone here. In her last days, she made me promise to reach out to you again. Knowing that now you were an adult and there was a possibility that things may be different. That now you would be able to make your own choices about whether you wanted me in your life. She knew I needed your forgiveness.'

'Hang on,' I interrupted. 'You said, Theresa encouraged you to reach out to me *again*. You never reached out to me. Ever. You just left and that was it. I never heard from you until I saw you standing there at the end of my hospital bed.'

'I feared that may have happened. I sent letters and, for what it's worth, presents, over the years. But I never heard back from you. Your mother, through her lawyers, made it very clear that you didn't want anything to do with me. I didn't realise she had not passed anything on to you. I don't blame her. She was hurting and she wanted to hurt me and maybe protect you. Who knows? I suppose I could have tried harder, but I felt such guilt about leaving you, that I understood and sadly accepted that you did not want anything to do with me. I saw it as my punishment, karmic'.

In that moment, my heart broke for the loss. The

loss of what could have been. The loss of the opportunity to have lived my life differently, without so much destruction and dysfunction. If only I had known that he did care. That at least, I meant enough for him to write to me. I never knew this and therefore I never felt he cared. She took this from me. Why did *she* take this from me? It could have all been different. Maybe it wouldn't have been. But the chance, the slightest possibility that it could have been was simply too much for me to process. All the pain, self-hatred, self-abuse and struggle might never have needed to exist.

My grief overwhelmed me. And it took me into a deep sadness for days. Beneath the sadness lay a simmering bubble of deep dark resentment towards my mother. As an adult, I had appeased any disharmony I felt towards her, by feeling sorry for her. She was weak, she was quite pathetic and she just hadn't known how to cope with life—she had never really known how to cope with life— that, in a way, justified her behaviour, her lack of being the mother I needed her to be.

But this knowledge, that she had withheld my father from me, opened-up a whole new wound. A painful wound that was just too immense to deal with. Another layer, had revealed itself, but I was not ready or able to deal with this.

I shut down.

FEELING INTO
THE DARKNESS

As a heaviness and darkness, fell over me again, I felt
the urge to run. But I did not run. I felt the urge to drink.
But I did not drink. I felt the urge to cut myself. But I did
not cut myself. I felt the urge to get high. But I did not get
high. I felt a desperate need to make it all go away again.
But I did not make it go away again.

This time it *had* to be different. This time I felt my
way through the darkness. Guided by my father's gentle
hand. I didn't know where this whole journey I was on
was going to end. I didn't know what it was going to look
like. I didn't know who I was going to be at the end of it.
I knew that now, in this place, at this time, was exactly

where I had to do it. The reappearance of my father in my life was the key. He told me, that he knew he must go to me that day and he did. He found me and brought me home. Home to heal. Home to find my home.

He had woken that morning, after dreaming of me, to feel a presence with him: a presence, who he knew to be Theresa. She had been with him often since she had passed. It gave him great comfort to be with her. To feel her. To reconnect with her. And he knew her presence that morning after he had dreamt of me, meant that the day had arrived when he had to find me. He had to heal his relationship with me. He'd tracked down my mother by phone and when he spoke with her, she was hysterical telling him that I had attempted suicide and was in a coma, and it was all his fault. He left his home that day and flew to my bedside. Returning to me, after all those years.

This remarkable man, who had done so much to heal himself, who had found himself along the way and who, through his own journey, helped so many others. I know he reappeared that day, not by chance, I know he was there that day, so that he could help me. Help me to find my way back.

I could not abandon him and more importantly, I could not abandon myself, not again. By forgiving my father, I had opened the door for him to forgive himself. In turn, I opened the door to heal myself, as painful and as traumatic as it was panning out to be, I knew I had to stay with it. I knew I couldn't run any more. His gentle guiding light, kept burning low, illuminating the path for me, especially as the darkness descended upon me.

The darkness lingered for many weeks. I was conscious of sitting with it, as my father had guided me. Trusting that when it was time to release it, I would know. I was so used to blocking it, ignoring it, hiding it, that this was an incredibly challenging period for me. The sadness and grief was overwhelming at times. I cried bucket loads of tears. More tears than I thought possible. Once the tears came out, I would fall into a heavy exhaustion and sleep, the deepest of sleeps. Healing sleeps. It was during these deep healing sleeps, that the dreams began. Dreams that I did not want to have. Because when it became a dream, it felt like it was no longer mine. It felt like it had escaped from the treasure chest that I had held it in for all these years. I wanted to hold it there, not let it become real, not even in a dream. When I would wake from the dreams... *he* would still be with me. I still felt him with me and I needed him to *not* be with me, because I did not have it within to handle him. I had worked too hard to hide him away from the world.

I had worked way too hard, to hide him away from me, for his memory to suddenly reveal itself now, in the middle of all that I was experiencing, all that I was already trying to process. It was challenging enough, this journey I was on, without him escaping. Escaping from the treasure chest deep within my soul where I had carefully held it for so long. That is where it was safe.

Every night he came to me. Every night I would

relive that night. That night that remained a complete mystery to me and every morning I would wake feeling a surge of ecstasy, coupled with an anxiety that I could not let it come out. I would do whatever I could to reverse that feeling of euphoria that would buzz within my waking body. I didn't want to remember that feeling. Remembering that feeling and wanting that feeling had only brought enormous disharmony and dysfunction into my life. Why can't I remember to forget you?

I awoke one morning, with this same sensation of euphoric bliss engulfing me and I heard the words, *Stay with it*. I thought I was awake, but I am not sure that I was, because what transpired after this felt completely surreal and dreamlike.

'I don't know how. I don't know how to stay with it.'

Allow yourself to just be with it. Stop fighting Halia. Breathe into it.

'I can't. I'm scared to go there.'

You don't have to go there. There is no there. There is only here. And here is within you. It is within you. It has always been within you. You must learn to allow it while you are here.

'I don't know how to learn it. I tried to find it, in every way possible, and it was never enough. I don't want to go there again. I am scared. What if I can't find it here? What if I can't allow myself to feel it here? Then I will have to go back searching for it again and look how that turned out.'

Yes, but this time the search will be within you. You

were looking for it outside of you. You must now find it within you.

'Show me how. If I am to find it, tell me how I am to find it.'

Give your time. Give your focus. Give your thoughts to others. Take them away from yourself and give to others, to children. You must trust and listen—listen and trust—you are loved.

There was silence as I opened my eyes to the ceiling of my room. The ceiling fan turning rhythmically making patterns in the rays from the sunrise which danced on the ceiling.

I felt still. I felt calm. I felt bliss. Not the giddy overwhelming ecstatic bliss. Just a calm, still bliss and I liked it. It felt new and I felt safe.

I moved through the next couple of days in this state of calm. Comfortable in the stillness that was within myself. I arranged to volunteer at the local elementary school. Over the years, my father had worked closely with the school, helping children who needed support. More than what school could offer and because of this I was quickly able to secure a volunteer role, assisting in an integration program for pre-schoolers'. They only attended two days each week, which provided me with enough time to continue to do my other work as my father referred to it.

I called it sitting on the beach staring into the beauty of the ocean before me.

I called it walking up mountains.

I called it cooking.

I called it sitting in silence.

He called them healing: therapeutic. I knew that he must be right, because I was changing. I did not know how and I did not know what I was changing into, but it had to be better than I was before, right?

STICKY TAPE

Children were not really my thing. I didn't *do* kids as a rule. That was one problem with Christopher. He wanted children and I didn't. A fundamental problem, when one considers it, but I suppose I just avoided it and said I was concentrating on my career and I had plenty of time. But he knew, and I knew, I never had any intention of going there. I'm not sure why.

Here I was, surrounded by four-year-olds, who in fact, were quite sweet and funny. My role was to simply help, play with them, do activities with them, prepare what was needed for the day, clean up when they finished. Help them if they needed help. It was simple and I liked it.

One day, a few days in, as I wiped the paint from a

table, a little boy, a very sweet, yet somewhat different little boy, came up to me and declared, 'I'm dowing to det you some icky tape for Kismas.'

'Oh, aren't I lucky, you are going to get me some sticky tape for Christmas. But why would I need some sticky tape for Christmas my little friend?'

'So, you can ick you back togefer.'

'Right, I see. I need to stick myself back together. But I'm not broken little man,' I laughed waving my arms and legs around in front of him.

'Yes, you are,' he countered. 'You are broken on the inside. I tan see it in your eyes.'

'Oh!' I was stunned by both his forthright nature and his insight.

'It's OK but, acause my mumma, she fixes people that are broken on the inside. She can fix you,' he smiled and walked away.

I sat on the edge of the table dumbfounded. My ego trying desperately to berate the arrogance and rudeness of the child, my inner voice gently reminding me to listen and trust.

A day later, I watched the little man's mother come to pick him up. I did not know how she fixed 'people that are broken on the inside', whether she was a psychologist, a doctor or some other sort of healer. She looked very normal and as I watched her lovingly engage with her little boy, I felt a quite assuredness come over me, giving me the confidence to approach her.

'Hello,' I walked towards her. Her smiling eyes

flickered up to my face. I wonder if she was reading my body like her little boy did. I wonder if she could see just by looking at me that I was broken on the inside? If she could, her face, nor her eyes gave it away.

'Hello, I am Tabitha, Zac's mother.'

'Lovely, to meet you. I'm Halia, and I'm helping out here for a few weeks.'

'Oh, that is fabulous. I hope my little man was very good for you this morning,' she laughed tussling her son's mop of white blonde hair.

'I was mumma. I was dood. I'm always dood,' proclaimed Zac. 'Mumma, Halia, she's broken. You need to fix her!'

I laughed. Tabitha looked slightly embarrassed yet bemused at the same time.

'Zac darling, why don't you go and play for a few minutes with the other children, while mummy and Halia have a chat.'

'Yay!' Zac squealed as he raced off to play some more. I loved the simplicity of children. They were excited and content with the little stuff and they innately knew how to just be within themselves and play and enjoy the moment. There was much I could learn from these children and maybe I already had. Here I was standing in front of a stranger about to discuss my brokenness, something I had tried desperately to keep hidden from the world for a very long time. Yet, here was a child, who had simply spoken his truth without concern for what anyone thought, or, oblivious to what anyone thought. I loved that he was still so unaffected by 'life' that he was still able to live in his truth. Free from all the emotional baggage; the conditioning, the social constraints of life. I looked at the way he was playing, with not a worry in the world. Free to just be. Just be exactly who he was. I envied him in that moment. Because I wanted that again. It had been so long since I allowed myself to be in my truth without concern for what anyone thought.

I turned back to Tabitha, not sure of how long I had been staring into the playground watching the children, deep in my own thoughts. I became acutely aware that Tabitha was looking at my face. Deeply looking at my face. Had she been watching me the whole time? Suddenly, I felt extremely uncomfortable. Almost naked standing in the playground. I felt exposed.

'I must go,' I stammered.

Tabitha, gently touched my arm to stop me from walking away.

'I am sorry. Sorry if I made you uncomfortable. I do not normally do that, not here, in a space like this.'

Even though I didn't really know what it was she was referring to doing, I did understand and feel comforted by the authenticity of her apology. *Listen and Trust. Trust and Listen.*

'So, word on the street, well, according to your little man, is that I am in dire need of sticky tape for Christmas, to fix all my broken bits.'

'Oh, I am sorry, if Zac offended you by his bluntness.' Again, she gently touched my arm. 'He does have an extraordinary gift for being able to read people, and he hasn't quite figured out the social rules about when and how it is appropriate to use his gift. But I don't want to stifle him in anyway and make him feel that what he is, is in anyway wrong, by conditioning him by the what is and is not socially acceptable. Rightly or wrongly, I want him to hold onto who he is and his wonderful uniqueness for as long as possible. Truth be told, I hope he never loses it. I hope the 'rules' never get in. I hope he holds onto his true self forever, so he doesn't have to wander down the sometimes hard and lonely path re-finding himself. The path I have been on. The path that you are on, Halia?'

I wish she was my mother. I wish I was told it was okay to be me when I was a child. I wish I had held onto me. I wish I hadn't had to go through so much pain and anguish trying to find me again. The me, that I had lost somewhere along the way. That desperate quest I had been on without even knowing it, had not found or taken me back home to me, it had left me completely and utterly broken. The unravelling of the mess I had created, was quite simply exhausting, and I feared a never-ending task.

'Yes,' Tabitha said interrupting my thoughts, and again gently touching my arm. 'It can seem like a mountain that feels so huge and near impossible to reach the illusive peak. Sometimes it feels easier to just give up and stop trying.'

I nodded astounded by how she had read my thoughts.

'I don't want to give up. I don't want to stop trying. I am determined to get to the top of my mountain. I believe I can. I'm just at a loss as to the 'how' sometimes.'

'Listen and trust. Trust and listen, Halia,' Tabitha paused looking intently into my eyes, smiling. 'That is what you have done. And it has brought you to this moment and I think I am your *how* for now, if you will allow me to work with you?'

I was overwhelmed by this interaction I had found myself innately drawn to.

'Of course, I will allow you to work with me. How could I possibly not work with you? It's like you already know me better than I know myself!' I laughed at the absurdity and yet pure divinity of the moment.

Again, she touched my face ever so gently, and pulled me into a beautiful motherly hug saying, 'Let's meet tomorrow afternoon, when you finish work here, at the beach. We can chat to start with.'

'Sure.'

'Now,' she said, with a little shake of her head. 'Back to being a mum. Where's that little man of mine?' She strolled into the playground gathering Zac in her arms and swinging him around joyfully.

That is how I met Tabitha. The woman who was to change my life, by guiding me further up that mountain and helping me to overcome whatever blocks I came across along the way. To help me to find the courage and confidence to keep going. To keep digging. To keep growing. Sometimes I wonder. Does the summit really exist? Or, do we just keep going and find comfort and peace and acceptance in where we are on the mountain? Am I 'me' my true self, only when I get to the top? Or, am I 'me' my truth at all times? Am I 'me' at the bottom of the mountain as much as I am at the top of the mountain, if that exists at all? None of that really mattered, because the truth was, I just wanted to find peace within myself and feel at one with myself. I didn't care where on a mountain that was and how I found it.

I just knew that I had to find it. I had to find my way home.

TABITHA'S STORY

The first time that I saw Halia, was a week or so before I met her in person. I watched her interacting with the children when I came to pick up Zac. I often liked to hide inside and sneak a peek into my little man's world to see how he was interacting with others; to see who he was in this space.

He was a little different, my darling boy. He knew things, that perhaps a child is not supposed to know. But it was not through my teaching, he had just remembered. Remembered things from his past experiences and they were here with him and he had a deep knowing and that ability to intuitively know other's souls. He is yet to realise that this is not how everyone else views the world, and so lives within his truth without hesitation. It can be a lonely path to walk, having such knowing and the gifts that he has.

I too have this gift. I always have.

As a child, I knew when my mother walked into the room, if she was happy or sad, angry or joyous, scared or at peace. It was a good thing to know because she was very up and down with her emotions, it was like walking on egg shells. Now, as an adult, I know that she probably would have been diagnosed as bi-polar, but she never was.

Understandably, life could be a little tricky. As the oldest, I saw it as my job to protect my younger siblings, all three of them, from her. Not that she ever meant harm. I know that, but she did not know how to manage her emotions and at times it could be chaotic.

The first time I remember reading her, I was about four years old, I saw her walk into the kitchen and I could feel her anger. It is hard to articulate, because it is not something I saw in her—I could simply feel the energy and I knew what it was—it was like a voice within me. A familiar voice that spoke to me every night as I was going to sleep, who told me that she was angry and I knew that I needed to make sure that my younger brother and baby sister were out of her way, so they did not make her angrier. I knew in that state the littlest thing could trigger her and result in an outburst.

I had been on the other end before, and I knew that I had to keep my sibling's safe, so I gently coaxed them back into the bedroom and kept them quite with stories and cuddles.

I soon learnt to also keep a stash of food hidden in the bedroom as it could sometimes be hours, before the darkness of her mood would lift and food helped bribe my brother and baby sister to stay quiet. This continued for many years. It was a huge responsibility to carry and it became a burden, heightened by my ability to read people and see into the depth of their soul as soon as I met them. It became overwhelming and as a result I became increasingly anxious during my childhood.

Often, I did not want to know. Because it was too scary, what I saw in others.

Like the time, my mother brought home a man who we did not know, which sadly she often did when she was in one of her manic states. As soon as he walked into the house, I could see a cold evil darkness within him. I was about eight at the time, we still had a baby sitter with us then, but by the time I was nine or ten, I was left in charge of the children, while my mother would go out at night.

This was her pattern, when she was in her darkness she would stay home, barely leaving her room. Which was horrible and not pleasant to be around, because her darkness brought her anger and resentment towards us to the surface. We each represented, a man in her life, who had hurt and betrayed her, and so in those times of darkness it felt like she would take revenge on our fathers through us. So, bitter was her soul.

Yet, in some ways it was almost easier to be in that space, because at least I knew what I was dealing with and could manage things with the little ones to minimise the turmoil. When she got out of her dark phase and became the polar opposite, she would lavish us with love and seek forgiveness and go above and beyond to be this extraordinary mother. But high on life, she would also love to be out partying and meeting people, mostly men. And they would often end up at home with her. This was not new. I had experienced it my whole life.

On this night, I both saw and felt the evil in this man's soul. I clung hard to the baby sitters leg, silently begging her to stay. But she didn't want to be in that space as much as I didn't. She uncurled me from her leg, touched my face gently and walked away. Did I blame her? Maybe I did. I think I blamed a lot of people. All those who knew what was going on in our home and never did anything to help us.

Not only could I sense a person's energy, I also saw flashes of their story. I receive pieces of information, which I quickly integrate to formulate a picture in my mind's eye. I liken it to a jigsaw puzzle and as the data comes to me and the jigsaw comes together, the picture becomes clear. In some instances, frighteningly clear.

As the baby sitter left, and this man looked at me fearfully standing there, I saw flashes of his story and I had to stifle a scream, because I was so afraid by what I saw. I was a child and what I saw him doing to other children was terrifying. I felt he knew that I could see that, because he smirked at me, almost mocking me. I took myself into my bedroom, after my mother lavished me in kisses and declarations of love. When I heard, them go into her bedroom, I crept back out to the kitchen and grabbed the biggest knife that I could. I went into my brothers' room, taking my two sleepy little sisters with me. They were quite use to 'being quiet' when I instructed them. They knew it was the only way they could stay safe. And never did it seem more important.

I told my brother, who was only twelve months younger, what I had seen, and told him to get his baseball bat ready. We snuggled together, while the little ones slept safe in his bed. It was like we were on night watch. Waiting anxiously, readied for the attack I had forseen. When we heard the footsteps, we jumped up and stood in the doorway, he with his baseball bat and me with the kitchen knife. I mustered every ounce of courage I could find, and like a warrior set for battle I steadied myself, eyes solely focussed on that door. As it opened, his eagerness to get inside and fulfil his vulgar desires was palpable and I curbed the purge of disgust that surged through me, holding myself, with a steely fearlessness which I felt from the depth of my core.

'You take one more step into this room, I swear to God I will kill you and cut off your filthy vulgar penis and stick it in your own mouth, you filthy fucking paedophile.'

It was a voice that was not mine, yet the words were coming out of my mouth. I was eight years old and didn't consciously know what a paedophile was, nor was I in the habit of talking about penis' or swearing. But it came from me, from a powerful force within and I believed in it. I felt many other energies around me, supporting me. I felt powerful and safe, which made me feel bizarrely calm in the most frightening of situations.

Here we were just two small children in our pyjamas with tasselled bed hair, holding a knife and a baseball bat. In truth, we were no threat to him, but I know he felt something because he paused and looked slightly alarmed. There was a silent stand-off for a moment, as he obviously was deciding what his next move would be. His desire for one or all of us, was obviously strong because he took another step forward. At which time, from nowhere I raised the knife in the direction of his throat.

'Do not take one more step. I know what you have done to Timothy Vasils and little Brett Pierce and Samantha Moore. I know the vileness that you have done to them, I have seen it. So, get the fuck out of here now.'

He paused, fear and confusion entering his eyes, and then he smirked with disdain as he looked at me.

'You're as mad as your fucking mother. The whole town knows it. You little witch. Burn in hell witch. Burn in hell.'

'Yeah, maybe I will,' I responded feeling beyond powerful. 'And I have no doubt I will see you there. Now get out and never come back.'

When I heard the front door slam, I fell to my knees and vomited all over the carpet. My brother cradled me and I could smell the urine coming from his drenched pants and I heard the little ones murmuring and stifling their hysteria for fear of our mother hearing.

There were other situations like this, none quite as dramatic, but still scary. I told my mother what had happened, but in her manic state she did not want to believe it, she wanted to hold her blissfully happy state for as long as she could. And facing a truth like that would be stepping into her responsibility to protect us, but at her core, she did not know how to protect us and she honestly resented us most of the time anyway.

By the time, I was thirteen I was exhausted on every level of my being, from physically looking after my siblings and mentally needing to be on high alert most of the time. Emotionally, I was a ball of anxiety, which I covered well from the outside world, as I had to stay on top of things. I had to stay in control. I simply couldn't fall in a heap. Energetically, I was a mess. Of course, I did not know it at the time, but my gifts had become a burden to me, because I was seeing and knowing and feeling so much of other peoples, from my family, to my friends, to my teachers, to just random strangers walking down the street. And I was carrying much of their 'stuff' because I did not know how to protect myself energetically. I was not taught how to manage my energy or how to wisely use my gifts.

It was very lonely being me. I could not share this with anyone. I know people felt I was different, because of how they would look at me and sometimes kids would say things, obviously having heard their parents talking about me.

While most times, I would see and feel things within

people, and not say anything, there were times, when I felt compelled to say things, even though I knew what they would think of me. Like when I would see cancer growing in people, or flashes of an abusive partner, or a child being abused. This knowing would haunt me, as I knew I could make a difference to their life, if they knew what I knew. I was not sure within myself whether I was supposed to tell them or not. Most often, as I said, I would not, but in serious situations: I felt a deep sense of responsibility to say something to them.

I suppose this added to the silent whispers around town about me. It was a small town, an unforgiving, judgemental and very religious town. I would try and be as discreet as possible, so I did not show myself as the 'witch' I was rumoured to be. I remember, telling a teacher that she should go and see her doctor about her 'woman's parts', as I had seen cancer in her cervix. Another time, I gave a domestic violence support card to the local pastor's wife. I had seen the knife that he had held to her throat. I knew exactly what he was doing to her at home, when he was not standing on his pulpit preaching about goodness and condemning others for their sins. And then there was the time, when I was fourteen, when I simply had to tell one of my friend's mothers, that she needed to ask her daughter what was going on each night at home, while she was at work. I had seen my friend's stepfather sexually abusing her, and I saw her shrivelling up inside and closing herself off from the world. I saw her constant suicidal thoughts and I had to help her. Her mother, who was a venomous woman, told me to mind my own business and to keep my little 'witch nose' out of things. Sadly, and quite traumatically for me in these circumstances, I was often told to mind my own business.

When my friend, finally did commit suicide only a week after I spoke to her mother, something changed in me.

At her funeral, her mother came up to me and stared me in the eye and brutally whispered to me, 'I know you did this to her. I know you got inside my precious girl's head and cursed her with your evil. Leave now, you are not welcome here.'

I recall looking at the people around me and while none of them had heard what she said, I could see what they were all thinking about me and it scared me. It scared me right out of my truth.

I shut it all down that day. I blocked it completely. I now know that my soul, my whole energetic self, went into shock, and any connection to my truth, my inner self was blocked by a fear so deep and old. I began to live my life from a different place. I suppose I fitted into how they all wanted me to be.

How my mother wanted me to be. Nobody wanted a witch as a daughter.

How my friends wanted me to be. Nobody wanted a witch as a friend.

How my teachers wanted me to be. Nobody wanted a witch as a student.

How that small-minded town wanted me to be.

Nobody wanted a witch in their town.

History has told us this and I consoled myself with the thought that it was safer for me to be what they wanted me to be and I became completely empty inside. Part of me died. I was lonely: not like before when no one understood me. This was a deeper loneliness. I was missing a part of myself. My truth.

My brother was the only one who saw what was happening to me and he tried to coax me back out, concerned for me. I valued his love for me, but I could not allow myself to open to that truth again. It was too painful. Everyone else seemed pleased that I had ditched my gifts and become normal. They could all sleep happier at night knowing I was fitting in their little square box, where they felt comfortable.

Until, my little man was born. And then everything changed.

I had left the small-minded town as soon as I finished school, which was refreshing. And then when I was pregnant with Zac things started to change and I started to feel less empty. Less lonely. Those ten years had been very dark and lonely. But I felt myself breaking through some of this in my pregnancy. While labouring, a beautiful peaceful labour, if there can be such a thing, I became so in tune with my body and the energy flowing within it. It felt incredibly intimate in that space with just me, my body and my baby. I worked with my body, with that amazing connection to my energetic body to birth my son. And, in birthing my son, I birthed myself, my true self once again.

This time, I made sure that I got help, wisdom and sage advice from others who were not afraid of my truth and who understood me, who I really was. In that, I gained acceptance and an understanding of how to work with my gifts and how to protect myself in the process.

I've been doing this for the past four years, while raising Zac. I now understand my gifts and I nurture them and I have learnt how to use them to help other people, like my beautiful friend Halia.

I trust that those whom I am supposed to work with, will find me, just as Halia found me, with a little help from my little man!

LAYING THE
FOUNDATIONS

We began our work, meeting on the beach one afternoon. We sat together, with our feet in the sand and chatted. At least, that was what I thought was happening, that we were just chatting. While I spoke about why I am working with the children, and why I am here in Hawaii, and about my dad and learning to surf, and quite light surface level things, my beautiful new friend, was sitting analysing my soul through her inner dialogue which I had no idea she was doing. I was still quite oblivious to the depth of who *I* was.

It is important for me to get to know the person

that I am working with, and the best way to do that, is to have a chat. But it is also a way for me to start to get more of a feel for the person's energy and where some of their problems are coming from. Not from that surface level, they are just the reflection or manifestation of the true imbalance within the soul.

I could see that things within Halia were already shifting. That she had started to do her work. But there was still a lot of congestion of sorts within the energetic field. I knew that before we went digging too deeply, Halia needed a greater awareness of her energetic self. She was on this path, in her own way, but was a little directionless, not knowing where to go next or in fact, what she was doing on the path. It was her healing path, but she really had no idea what she was doing within herself on an energetic level. Changes had begun to occur within her energetic body, but they were not integrating fully and she was not grounding herself in those changes, so there was a chance that they would not hold or stick, when she was faced with similar situations again or when facing the same people again.

After a long pause, Tabitha spoke. 'We will begin our work together, by daily yoga practice followed by short periods of meditation.'

Of course, I had no idea of the bigger picture. I thought that Tabitha just invited me to her yoga classes as yoga would be good for me—it was going to be good for me physically—but really, I didn't know that it had nothing to do with the physical. Her intention, was for me to start to come in-tune with my own energetic self, and start my stagnant energy flowing again, allowing all the work that I had done since I had been here, to integrate. Every time, we finished our yoga and meditation session, I would walk away feeling more connected and grounded in myself.

Physically I felt great. It was great to use my physical body in a gentle way for once. For this yoga was very gentle. I did want to try the heated power flow type yoga as I knew I would love the intensity of it, the challenge of it, but Tabitha discouraged this, as she knew that I would find a false escape from myself, in the intensity of this type of yoga. She explained to me, gently yet firmly, that it was no longer about escaping from myself, it was about finding myself and knowing myself.

When we move slowly, in these ancient poses, our energy begins to flow in the way it is meant to flow. There is purpose in the practice, in practicing the pose, but more so in practicing the connection you have to yourself in that moment of being present with your body. When there is nothing else, but you, your breath and the movement of your body, it is a beautiful experience. And to watch Halia transition, from seeing her yoga practice as a physical pursuit, to using it as a point of connection to herself was beautiful. She needed a tool to connect to herself, and she found this in yoga. Each practice, she opened a little more, and we would take that beautiful time afterwards to meditate together, for short periods to start, and then longer periods, where the new opened energy pathways would settle and she would become grounded in this state of being.

Halia needed this awareness and connection to her energetic self, before we could start the deeper level of healing. I had seen within her brokenness, that she needed this foundation before we did any other work, or it would be too intense for her and she would run away. I had seen it with people I had worked with before. If people are not ready for the intensity of the healing work that I do, then they will sabotage it and reverse it, taking themselves back to where they are comfortable: a place of discomfort in their old ways. But for some, that is where they prefer to be, until they are ready to do their work, if they are ready to do their work in this life. And they may not be. And that is okay too. Their soul healing will always be there for them, whether it is this life, or the next.

Once I realised this, I knew that I wanted to do my work in this life. I wanted it to be done. Tabitha cleverly set up a strong foundation for my healing work to begin on a whole new level, through my yoga and meditation practices and I was ever so grateful for that foundation. Because when we began digging and healing, my foundation was rocky, but I was glad that it existed and I used my yoga and meditation to keep me grounded as we delved deeper into my soul and her pain.

I could have run away, that first day that I lay on the table in Tabitha's treatment room. I was confronted and it was so painful, that I wanted to jump from the table and run away. But I chose not to. Because I trusted her.

The first thing asked as I lay there was, 'Tell me about your mother? Why do you hate your mother?'

I simply did not know where to begin. In a way, the last couple of weeks, working with the children and concentrating on my yoga and meditation with Tabitha, was a beautiful and a welcomed distraction from my own persistent thoughts and emotions and now here I was about to face them again and part of me didn't want to.

As if reading my mind, Tabitha said, 'I know you do not want to go there. But you must, because it will not go away until you do and all that hate will keep showing up in your life. It is stopping you from being you and being happy. Let's release it. It's time.'

Convinced by her sincerity and having faith in her, I felt safe to go there. As she placed her hand on my belly button, the deep connection point between mother and child, and another on my heart, I closed my eyes and allowed myself to feel the despise for my mother surface.

'I hate my mother for taking away my happiness. For ignoring me. For not seeing me. For never being present. For not being there for me when I needed her. For not nurturing me. For lying to me. For keeping me away from my father. For being so sad and pathetic her whole life. For being weak. For not trying to fix herself. For giving up on herself. For opting out in life. For not being able to face life. For running away from life.'

I paused, not knowing where a lot of this had come from, feeling like I was bubbling with anger, about to explode.

Then, Tabitha placed one hand on my stomach and another on my forehead.

'Tell me why you hate yourself Halia?'

I didn't understand. I didn't hate myself. *Did I?* I didn't particularly love myself, but I wasn't sure that I hated myself. Tabitha sensed my resistance.

'Take a deep breath and allow it to come.'

I really did not want it to come. I really wanted this to be over. I didn't hate myself, not in the way I hated my mother. I just didn't like myself much, most times. I lay there waiting for Tabitha to move on as I believed she had missed the mark on this one, that she was heading down the wrong path, because I didn't really hate myself. *Did I?*

'That's fine sweet, just take your time. It will come when it is ready. Just breathe, a few more deep breaths,' encouraged the ever-patient Tabitha, again sensing my thoughts. I felt irritated and uncomfortable on the table and started wriggling around a little, trying to stretch out the discomfort I was feeling develop across my shoulders and in my chest.

'Just breathe. It's okay.' Tabitha guided me.

Annoyed now by her persistent gentleness I snapped,

'I don't want to breathe okay!'

'Why. Why don't you want to breathe?'

'If I breathe then it will come and I don't want it to come. I am scared for it to come. Because it is one thing for me to hate my mother. It is another for me to hate myself. I know I can get to the point of forgiving my mother. But I don't know if I can ever forgive myself.' I shouted, so irritated.

'Why can you never forgive yourself?'

I felt a wave of emotion roll over me. A tsunami of emotion coming from nowhere and there was nowhere to hide.

'I cannot forgive myself because I am so much more pathetic than my mother. I am so much weaker. I am such a hypocrite. I criticise her for running away from life and yet I am the one who has run away from life. I am the one who opted out of life on every level. I am the pathetic weak one. I am the one who has blamed everyone else and stuck my head in the sand. I am the one who used drugs to block my pain. I hate myself, because I am my mother, yet I am worse than her because at least she owned it. I just sat in judgement while I did the same thing and just tried to blame everyone else for why I was so fucked up. Why have I always been so fucked up?'

'So, why do you hate yourself?

'Because I'm a hypocrite. Blaming everyone else for their failings and not facing my own pathetic life and using everything I could get my hands on to stop me from facing it.'

'Who else do you blame?' This time Tabitha put her hands on my liver.

Oh yeah, that liver could do with some healing hands, with all the drugs and alcohol I have pumped through it.

'It's not really about the drugs and alcohol. Your liver is where you hold all your resentment, bitterness and anger.' Tabitha explained, again reading my thoughts.

And with her hands on my liver, I felt that anger. The hatred that had been bubbling for the last little while started to explode through my body. My whole body started to tremble and it felt like I had pins and needles pulsing through my limbs. My hands felt like they were exploding, my throat constricted and my lips were so electrifyingly numb, I could barely talk. I didn't know what was happening, but convinced myself I was safe and that it was just energy being released and that I could not fight it any longer.

'I blame them all. My mum, my dad, my sister, my friends, my teachers, my husband, my mother-in-law, my boss. All of them.'

'Why do you blame them?'

'For not helping me. I needed help and no one helped me!'

'Didn't they all try to help you?'

'No, they let me struggle and never helped, they all just made it worse!' My throat tightened more as I told this untruth. 'No,' I conceded, 'I suppose they all did try in their own way to help me, I just didn't let them.'

'Why didn't you let them help you?'

'I didn't want to be helped. I wanted to struggle.'

'Why did you want to struggle?'

'I deserve to struggle. I only deserve to struggle. I've screwed up and I don't deserve to have anything more than struggle. I don't deserve to be happy!'

'Okay. So, who do you really blame?'

'I blame me. I blame me for screwing up,' I sobbed with the realisation that I had not let myself acknowledge this before now.

Tabitha took her hands from my body.

'Let's find out why you are really blaming yourself, why you are punishing yourself in this life and why you're not allowing yourself to be happy. Let us find what it was that you did that makes you think that you screwed up. And it has nothing to do with this life.'

Taking a deep breath, I prepared myself to go even deeper. For what she said, I just knew to be true. I had been on a self-destructive path for so long and I never really understood why I had so intensely sought to destroy myself. There was something I longed for, which was that crazy ecstasy feeling, but it was something I almost fought to keep myself away from in some screwed up kind of way. The more I chased that feeling, the further I took myself away from it. I realised this in some way but never understood why. Now I did, because on a deeper level, I did not believe that I deserved anything but struggle. I didn't deserve that amazing feeling. I deserved to be punished, not rewarded.

Placing her hands on my forehead, Tabitha instructed

me to close my eyes and to take us to that time in the past when I screwed up and had the belief 'I deserve to be punished' established in my soul.

As I began entering a meditative state, I started to see flashes of images but I could not understand them. Tabitha, connected to me and could access much clearer images and she gently talked me through the scene.

'I see you as woman. A mother. You are quite young. You seem to be happy but there is a deep sadness within you somewhere. You have a little one with you, playing nearby. A little boy maybe four or five years old. He is happy and cheeky. And then a man comes along. Your heart races a little more and your eyes sparkle with joy seeing him. He is your everything. He brihgs you so much happiness. You run to him and throw yourself into his arms. It feels like it is a long time since you have seen him. Like he has been away, for quite some time. You are overwhelmed with emotion. And you hold him close. Smelling him. Feeling him. Taking him in again. It has been a long time.

He takes you by the face and looks deep into your eyes. And everything feels okay again. Your sadness lifts and you allow yourself to feel that deep sense of peace and calm when everything settles back into place, the way it is supposed to be. You feel whole, complete and at peace. This feeling engulfs you and you shiver.

Then you break the moment, by saying, 'Come and meet your son'. You are so excited because he left before your child was born. You take your husbands hand and turn in the direction of where your son is playing.'

'Stop!' I scream sitting up heaving as the vomit brings itself into my mouth. Tabitha grabs the bin and I heave, emptying everything in my stomach. I sob and convulse again and again. Spit drips from my mouth, tears stream down my face.

Tabitha lovingly wipes my face, my mouth, my eyes and holds me. Enveloping me in her arms and allows the intensity of the feeling to subside. Strangely, I feel so much better and calmer. I know what is coming but I am okay with it. I am okay going there now.

And taking another deep breath, I lie back down and Tabitha again gently places her hands on my forehead. Again, I see images that I cannot quite piece together. One keeps flashing back again and again and it is the sight of the little boy; my son, I guess, lying face down in the water.

'You look to see your son, but you cannot see him. He is not where he was playing when you became distracted by your husbands return. You call his name. But when there is no response, you feel a little panic overcome you. You begin to look behind the trees, calling his name over and over. You run to the edge of the river along which you had been seated waiting and watching him playing. *He knows not to go to the river without me.* And, then you see him, lying face down in the water.

You freeze. Knowing you need to move but the shock keeps you rooted. Your husband rushes into the water and scoops up the child and returns to the edge of the river. You remain motionless, as if watching a dream. *This is not really happening,* you tell yourself. And then you race to your husband who is working desperately on your son, trying to revive him, but he could not have been in there for more than a few seconds you think, surely my back was turned for only a few seconds. *Or was it more?* You question yourself, remote from the scene playing out in front of you, *was I caught up in the world of reuniting with my love, distracted by my pure joy at having my husband home with me, safely, feeling content and complete for the first time in years. How long had I allowed myself to indulge in that feeling, while leaving my son to drown?* All these thoughts tumble through your head as your husband futilely attempts to revive your son. And the completeness that you felt only minutes ago is replaced by a deep dark emptiness, that you carried for the remainder of that life and sadly many lives in between, including this one.'

I sobbed with a deep sadness that I was so familiar with, yet could never understand. I cried tears of grief for all that had been lost, I guess in many lives, but especially in this one. For all the years, that I have punished myself and created struggle and pain in my life, I had held onto that empty feeling.

As my breathing settled and my tears subsided, Tabitha asked the question, 'When in this life did the belief that you deserve to be punished, become an active belief? Our beliefs are just energy, as are all our memories, thoughts and emotions, carried within our energetic body, *soul* if you will, from one lifetime to another. Much like the energy of our ancestors is carried within our DNA, from our physical appearance, to belief programs, character traits and their experiences. However, all our memories and beliefs are not actively impacting on our life. Something experienced in this life must trigger this energy for it to become activated. Much like a person may carry the cancer gene within their DNA, it does not mean that they will have cancer, unless external factors activate that gene.'

I pondered when in my life did this belief, that I deserved to be punished become active?

While I was reflecting on this on a conscious level, Tabitha was using one of her muscle testing techniques, to age recess me, to this time.

'What happened when you were nine years and three months old, Halia?' Tabitha asked.

I paused, it was all such a blur my childhood. I could not recall much of anything and then I remembered. My sister died. Rosie died exactly when I was nine years and three months old. *How had Rosie dying activated this belief in me? I was a kid, surely, I couldn't believe that I deserved to be punished for her dying.*

Tabitha explained, 'That while yes you were a child, in your physical body, your soul is never a child. Your soul felt responsible for Rosie. You saw yourself as responsible for looking after her, and saving Rosie in this life. Saving her again.'

'What do you mean, again?' I queried, not understanding.

'I feel. Sorry... I am being shown... that Rosie was your son in that previous life. Rosie's soul was your son's soul. And you selected her as your little sister in this life so that you could look after her and make good for what you saw yourself failing to do in that past life.'

'But I didn't do it. I didn't save her. I couldn't save her.' The grief and guilt overcoming me once more.

'And you were never supposed to,' explained Tabitha. 'Rosie was here to teach you. To teach you that you are not responsible for any one else's experience and to teach you to forgive yourself for what was done. To teach you to stop punishing yourself.'

It was too much. I went to anger, as I often do when I am emotionally overwrought.

'Fuck her or him or whoever they are. I didn't ask for her to come to teach me some lesson. All I know is that she was weird and I hated her. I hated her for getting sick and I hated her for leaving me. I didn't ask for a fucking lesson.'

'I know it feels like that, Halia, but on some level, you did ask for this lesson and in some way, you and Rosie had a soul contract, agreeing that this would be the way for you to learn the lesson.'

'Well that was a fucked-up plan wasn't it, because clearly I didn't learn the lesson and look at what I have done with my life. Look where I am!'

'Yes, look where you are at. You are here now, with me, learning this lesson. It may have taken a while, but it worked. You are learning and growing and coming home to your whole self for the first time in a long time. The first time in many lifetimes.'

While I heard, what Tabitha was saying, it felt quite

foreign to me. I was exhausted and I needed to process.

'I know you are exhausted, but now we have found and explored where the belief has come from, we have the chance to reverse this belief that continues to sabotage your life. Beautiful one, do you really want to continue to punish yourself for these things. These things, that you can clearly see, you are not responsible for. They may have happened decades ago or even lifetimes ago, but they are still impacting on you now, on your everyday. Haven't you inflicted enough pain on yourself over all these years?'

I reflected on all the ways I had punished myself over the years. From running until I would vomit, from studying until I couldn't keep my eyes open, from keeping friends and lovers at arm's length, to cutting myself, starving myself, drinking and drugging myself into oblivion for years, to destroying my marriage, the gentle yet seemingly purposeful sabotage of it simply because I was happy in it. Christopher did make me happy and I had to destroy it, because I did not deserve to be happy. And I suppose, my greatest punishment was in trying to take my own life. I really believed at that time, that I did not deserve to live. I did not want to live. I wanted the fastest and easiest way back there. But I wasn't allowed. I remember being sent back.

And now I am here.

I agreed to allow Tabitha to guide me through a limiting belief reprograming technique, where I changed my belief from 'I deserve *to* be punished' to 'I do *not* deserve to be punished' and 'I do *not* deserve to be happy' to 'I *do* deserve to be happy'. I understood that the vibration of these beliefs was now embodied within me. That belief was fundamentally a very different message that I was sending out into the universe. I no longer deserved to be punished and I deserved happiness.

What my life could hold if I was not attracting struggle and destruction.

PEAS IN A POD

I did little in the days following that life changing session with Tabitha. Allowing the changes to be processed and for everything to settle and I felt like it did, all except my sister. I was confused and upset by what had shown itself around her and I could not find peace when I thought of her. I knew there was more work to do, but I didn't know what or how.

She had died. I was a child. I don't really remember much else. So much had happened and besides I had sort of forgotten somehow. I think the pain of my parents abandoning me for her and their grief, was more painful than her passing.

We weren't alike. She was placid and sickly and *indoorsy*. I was robust and free and *outdoorsy*. That's how I remembered things. That's how I remembered my relationship with her. That's how I had forced myself to remember us, so that it was not so painful. If I was disconnected from her; different from her and hated her then it wouldn't hurt that she was gone. Well, that is what I had told myself, until now.

I soon learnt, that none of this was true and it was the story I had created to block my pain and the emptiness that existed within me when she left me. Everyone seemed to leave me and I think this is where it all began. The emptiness fuelling my search to be filled. Filled by anything or anyone, because without her, I didn't feel I was enough. She left me. So how could I ever have been enough?

I sat down in the sunshine with my father, on the front porch listening to the ocean. It had become our meeting place every morning, to connect and chat. On this morning, a few days following that session with Tabitha, I asked my father to tell me about Rosie. I valued and respected his incredible wisdom, having proven itself to me over the months that I spent with him after I left the hospital. I was learning so much. There was so much that I didn't remember about Rosie and me. So much that made my heart sing and cry at the same time.

He sat and told me stories. The childhood I had buried, because it was too painful to remember. If I remembered Rosie with anything but disdain, then I would potentially open this wound, so I had convinced myself that I hated her for going there, for leaving me here and for destroying my parents.

We sat long into the day, the tapestry of my childhood being rewoven with love, tenderness, compassion and a deep understanding of the love that I held for my little sister and the powerful love that she held for me.

My sister Rosie, was eighteen months younger than me. She had a silent wisdom, an inner calmness that balanced my wild free-spiritedness, my need to explore and expand. She was the grounding that I needed to function here, in those early scary days of being me. She was that ever-present calmness. I would return to her each afternoon after spending the day outdoors, and I would settle with her.

I would nurture and love her. And she would talk to me. Tell me stories. Her fairy-tale stories. The daydreams she would have while I was out living those dreams. We were two peas in a pod, so everyone would say. But never were there more different peas so comfortably matched, my father declared. It was the complete balance.

The Yin and the Yang.

The feminine to the masculine.

The soft to the hard.

The slow to the fast.

The calm to the storm.

The perfect harmony.

As little Rosie got sicker and sicker, she was not able to maintain her part in this harmonious dance we had established. The little twosome, who would fall asleep together every night, arms wrapped around one another began to split. As her health declined, she could not be there in that way I needed her. In the way, I had depended on her. My father told me she had to go to hospital and I could not stay with her. The first night she was away, I refused to go to bed. I threw a massive tantrum. I screamed and thrashed around until I had nothing left in me and then I went into some sort of self-enforced coma, not a physical coma, an emotional coma.

My father was only able to bring those memories to the surface, to stir them up, so that I could remember the emotion. The emotion of loving my sister. The feeling of being connected to my sister. The feeling of being complete, with my sister. All I could remember, was the feeling of nothing I enforced on myself, to protect myself. I hated going to the hospital to see Rosie, I remember this. I would not stay in the room. I could not talk to her and I could not be near her for long. I would just be there for as long as I was forced to by my parents and then I would wait out in the corridor, for hours, wanting to run away, to get away from where my little sister was disappearing before my eyes. But I couldn't run so I carefully cocooned myself, where nothing could get in and it didn't.

My baby sister died. My little Rosie died when she was only seven years old and I felt nothing. Other than a deep resentment towards her for leaving me. And leaving me empty. Leaving me feeling that I was not enough and that in some way I had failed her. Why did she have to leave me? Why do they all have to leave me for me to learn? Why didn't I learn sooner, so they didn't all have to leave me?

BREAKING THE DEPENDENCY

The intensity of my work with Tabitha died down a little. The first couple of weeks, once we really got stuck in the healing work—was very intense, and challenging—some sessions I had with her were so big and dug into these deep core issues and beliefs, other times, it was like just being in her gentle presence, grounded me and allowed all the upheaved energy to settle into place. I suppose she was like an anchor, where sometimes I just needed her energy to ground me and help me integrate all the big changes that were happening within.

Tabitha likened it to birthing. With all these changes in my beliefs, emotions and my awareness of everything,

I was becoming a different person. I was birthing a new me. During the birthing process sometimes it's intense, sometimes you need to retreat and allow it to happen within you and just be with it, and sometimes you need a helping hand to hold that space while you birth. Tabitha was my 'birth partner'.

I guess I became dependent on her for that. The healing process, once begun, can become quite addictive and that amazing connection that I had with her, made me want more of it. I think Tabitha sensed this, because she told me that she was going to Bali on a yoga retreat and she was to be away for two weeks, which seemed like an eternity to me, to be without her friendship and her energy, both of which I had become reliant on.

Again, in her wisdom, she told me. 'This time is important for you, Halia. It will give you the space you need to do your own work. You have it in you to heal yourself too, you know. You do not need me. And you need to discover this strength within yourself. You will see that you have enough within in you, you are enough!'

That felt so scary. Once again, I had allowed myself to become reliant on another and now she was leaving me as well. My go to reaction was anger, but this time I did not feel angry, because I now saw it differently. I saw that this was an essential part of my healing experience. I had to learn this.

She had brought me to this point, and now she was allowing me to walk the path alone for a little while. During our work, I had learnt many techniques to explore my subconscious, to connect with my inner self and to release unwanted energy in a healthy way. I had developed knowledge, skills and practices, that I never imagined in only a few short months, and it was time that I put them into practice, without the support of my beautiful friend and pseudo guardian angel.

I knew she would come back. I knew that she would not abandon me. I knew she was doing this as a wonderful loving gift to me. I was still a little scared. Did I really have it in me, to hold myself together? What if something big showed up and I didn't know how to handle it? What if I went back to the way I was when I couldn't handle things? What if I lost myself again after I had come this far? Yet I knew, that I had to experience life without Tabitha, to prove to myself that I could do it and this was the first time, that this was to be really tested. The first time the integrity of the new me was to be challenged. Was I enough without another to support me? There had always been someone or something to support me. To make me feel whole. To make me feel enough. And now it came down to me.

I began those two weeks, with discipline and a clear intention, that I would prove to myself that I was enough and I could hold my enoughness without Tabitha's energy.

Every morning I would wake at 4.30 am and I would meditate for half an hour. I was not so great at traditional meditation, as I had a very active mind. It was just getting into the habit of creating time and space to be still and be present with my inner self. As thoughts came up, I would notice them and then let them go. Sometimes, it was five minutes before I noticed that thoughts had crept in and that was okay, because then I would switch them off, and switch back into the nothingness, the stillness, the silence. And when I got there, I loved it.

When you have always had an extremely active mind, a mind that has dictated your life and created so much stress, it is so wonderful to finally be able to switch it off. Even if it was only for a minute at a time, before that next thought came in, it was bliss. The minutes of stillness, without the intruding thoughts had become longer, the more disciplined I had become with my meditation practice. It was practice, because like anything it takes time to develop a new skill, and yes, at times I was impatient and told myself I was not good enough and then I reminded myself that, that was the point. I was exactly enough with my mediation practice where I was, just as I was exactly enough with my yoga practice, just as I was exactly enough with my healing, where I was. In these times, Tabitha's words would echo in my ears, 'It is not a race. You are perfect where you are.'

After I finished my morning mediation, and before I would go to my yoga practice, I would journal. I'm not too sure what would happen in this space, I often just picked up a pen and would allow it to write. There would be pages and pages of ramblings, sometimes I would look over them, but often not. I think it was the process more than the content that was important to me. In writing this way, I suppose it was a subconscious way, because my mind was not an active participant in the process, I would experience a massive release of whatever had stirred up whilst I was sleeping and meditating.

I found it intriguing that it was in those practices of being still, that is sleeping and meditation, where so much came to the surface, almost like the bits and pieces of murky water rising to the top when the river is still. When the river is gushing and its flow chopping and changing, it is difficult for the murky bits to rise to the surface and be clearly seen. They just get caught up in the chaos of the torrents flowing, until there is stillness and silence, and then they can truly be seen. These were my subconscious thoughts and emotions. When I finally stopped, and silenced my mind and created stillness in my energetic body, all these low-lying thoughts, beliefs and emotions would show themselves and in my morning writing I would allow them to gently flow from me, exploring them, feeling them and then releasing them in the words that hit the pages before me. It was an incredible exercise, one I wish I had learnt years earlier, so that I may have been able to release the chaos and mayhem that was brewing with me.

There was still much work I needed to do on forgiving myself for the time that I had wasted or the time I believed that I had wasted. This was the focus of my work while Tabitha was away. I knew this and I admit I did try and avoid it for a few days. Busying myself after my yoga practice, with my volunteer job and then shopping for fresh produce and cooking beautiful food for the evening meal that I shared with my father. I had really begun to value those evenings, being with him, chatting to him, getting to know him. He was an extraordinary man, doing extraordinary meaningful, purposeful work. It all got me thinking about my life and whether the work I was doing in the past was purposeful. As a high-flying lawyer, the only purpose I attached to it at the time, was to make enough money to support the destructive lifestyle I had created for myself. Once I was with Christopher, my partying lifestyle died down, I suppose the only purpose was to maintain a social smokescreen that we were some sort of wealthy power couple. And it served that well.

But really what was the bigger purpose in my work? Was I changing the world with my work? To be honest with myself, I wasn't. There was those who work in my field who were using their position to help others and really change lives. My line of work, where I was supporting big business in minimising their legal risks during acquisitions and mergers was not, in my eye, changing the world! And, these thoughts stirred an anxiety in me. An anxiety about my future. What was I going to do with my life?

I reassured myself that I didn't need to worry, because there was no rush. I had plenty of time and fortunately I had plenty of money to continue to support myself here while I was not working. I was living simply, so I didn't need to worry. I pushed those little seeds of anxiety away somewhere within me. Ignoring them and telling myself I had plenty of time to worry about those sorts of things later. Once my work on me was done.

The following day, I was determined to delve into the forgiveness work I needed to do on myself. I found myself on the beach in the afternoon, and after a swim in the picturesque warm ocean, I decided it was time. I took my pen and paper and titled the page: I Forgive Myself For. After settling my mind and bringing myself into the meditative space I had become very familiar with, I was able to silence my conscious thoughts and allow my subconscious to take over. And then the words tumbled from me. The memories, splattered from my whole life— here and there, there and here—took over and fell onto the page.

I forgive myself for wasting money on drugs.

I forgive myself for destroying mums house.

I forgive myself for disconnecting from Rosie.

I forgive myself for abusing my body.

I forgive myself for wasting my life.

I forgive myself for hating my father.

I forgive myself for hurting Christopher.

I forgive myself for loosing myself.

I forgive myself for wasting so much time.

I forgive myself for being so naïve.

I forgive myself for judging others so harshly.

I forgive myself for keeping people at arm's length.

I forgive myself for abandoning Rosie when she needed me most.

I forgive myself for living *in*authentically.

I forgive myself for needing drugs to feel whole.

I forgive myself for needing Christopher to feel whole.

I forgive myself for losing myself.

I forgive myself for not letting others help me.

I forgive myself for wanting out of this life.

I forgive myself for trying to take my life.

I forgive myself for the pain I caused my mother.

I forgive myself for the pain I caused Christopher.

I forgive myself for not seeing my mother's pain.

I forgive myself for my selfishness.

I forgive myself for being so destructive.

I forgive myself for creating chaos in my life.

I forgive myself for all the struggle I created.

And, the list continued … as the tears poured. I sobbed, I gasped as these truths poured from me. The pain that I had brought upon myself and others ripping through my heart. Eventually, the pen stopped and I realised I had stopped crying as I felt a calmness descend upon me. I sat with it, digging my toes into the sand and really anchoring that blissful feeling of calm and peace within me. It felt perfect and I wanted to hold onto this simple, content and stillness that I had found.

I finished that afternoon with another beautiful swim and had not felt more alive in a long time. As I walked up the beach, a surfer approached me.

'Are you okay?'

'Yeah, I'm great thank you,' I could still feel that buzz.

'Oh great. Sorry, I noticed you were quite upset before and I wanted to check you were alright,' he stammered, in a strong Australian accent.

I hadn't noticed him, or anyone else on the beach while I was writing. I had become accustomed to being alone in what I regarded as my little corner on the northern end of the beach, which was normally quite private. Feeling slightly embarrassed at my raw vulnerability being witnessed, I assured him that I was in fact, completely fine and was just working through some stuff. I was not going to let embarrassment dampen my high.

'Okay great. That's good. I just wanted to make sure. See ya round.'

And off he strolled carrying his board. As I gathered my things together, I felt touched that this stranger had cared enough to check in on me. It was comforting to have someone care about me. Little did I know that this caring Aussie surfer was about to re-enter my life and turn my whole healing experience on its head.

MY WELCOME
DISTRACTION

That evening my father and I went for dinner at a local restaurant for my aunties birthday. I love that I had reconnected with people, who I had only met once as a small child, but they made me feel such a part of the family and I loved being part of a family. I suppose because mine had crumbled and I was never really accepted as part of Christopher's I did not really place value on the family unit. I was enjoying the sense of connectedness and unity that I felt I was a part of with my Hawaiian family. There was an ease with them, that I think came from the simple life that they had all continued to live, in this paradise. They had stayed in this gorgeous little town, all working to keep the town alive, surviving mostly on the surfing tourists who frequented all year around. My auntie ran a small hotel, and my cousins worked in that business. Another auntie had a gift shop in the main street that sold traditional touristy items as well as cool unique home décor, that she sourced from all over the world. One uncle worked on the local council, another was a teacher at the high school and had been for the last thirty-five years.

They had a simple life and they loved it. And I loved being a part of it. It brought me some sort of peace, knowing that my father had these people here for him, to help him to heal after he left Mum and I, all those years ago. Now, that I know how broken he was, I am grateful that he had these good solid people around him, to help him find his way. And, that was how I felt that night, surrounded by good solid people, who had accepted me without judgement and loved me simply because I was family and I did not feel I needed to prove myself. They did not ask questions as to why I was here, or how I was going. They just offered me unconditional love. It felt wonderful.

I admit that I was still glowing and elated from my huge release on the beach that afternoon and I felt a rare excitement brewing within me. I wasn't sure what this feeling was, or why it was there, but I liked how it felt and so when my cousins asked me if I wanted to go to the local bar, when dinner was finished, I thought, why not? I had not been out, since I had been here. I had preferred to stay in, with my father or alone in the evenings. Feeling too vulnerable to face the outside world when I first got here, and then choosing quite evenings and early nights to enable my early morning ritual that I had established since working with Tabitha.

As soon as I entered the bar with my cousins, I saw the Aussie surfer. We found a table and ordered some drinks. It felt good to be out and enjoying a glass of wine. This felt normal, and it felt good to try normal again. I didn't feel anxious or unsure of myself, I was still on that somewhat giddy high.

I was content with just one glass of wine and as I waited at the bar for my glass of mineral water, the Aussie surfer came and stood beside me. At first, he did not notice me, as he was talking to one of his friends behind the bar. It was often the case that the local surfers and visiting surfers would become great friends because they shared a passion for surfing, big wave surfing at that.

'Hey! I didn't see you there.'

'Hi,' I was a surprisingly a little nervous in my reply.

'Are you right for a drink?'

'Yeah, thanks I've just ordered.'

This all felt so strange and different to me. I had never felt uneasy talking to men. If a man had offered to buy me a drink, I had either taken him up on the offer if there was something in it for me, or I had told him where to go, in my tough girl stance. Now, I was neither of these girls. I had changed a lot. I suppose this was the first time the new version of me had been in this situation. I was softer, gentler and more vulnerable, which made me feel quite nervous.

Despite this uneasy feeling, I really liked the feeling of a male's attention, and there was something about his Aussie accent that triggered a longing deep inside. I was not sure where that was coming from, but I did not ignore it.

'So, were you okay on the beach this afternoon? I know you were doing your own thing, that's why I didn't interrupt you, but you seemed pretty upset.'

I laughed a little, embarrassed that my emotional rawness had been witnessed.

'Damn, I'll have to find a new spot. I didn't realise I was so exposed there. I've been going to that spot for months now and just chilling out, doing my thing and I've never seen anyone notice me. Of all the days to be noticed,' I laughed. 'Thanks for your concern. I'm okay. More than okay. I was just letting go of old stuff!'

'Yeah, I think you're more than okay too. And, you are a bit hard not to notice.'

I was so embarrassed and laughed as I felt myself blushing with his compliment. *Who was this blushing giggling girl?* I had never felt this girly, with a man. I played along, liking the feel of the dynamic flow between us. Me and this dark hair, blue eyed, broad shouldered Aussie surfer.

'Yes, hard not to notice, when I'm sobbing and blubbering, completely oblivious to the world around me,' I mocked myself.

'I like that. Being oblivious to all the world around you. Just being in the moment. That's where I am when I'm surfing. Not necessarily with the tears and the blubbering though, doesn't go down to well when you're sitting out the back waiting with the others.'

'So, are you a professional surfer, or just here trying to conquer our famous waves?' I tried to take the conversation away from me.

'Me, no way, not a professional. But I love coming here. I do it once every two years with my mates. We have for the last fifteen years. In the beginning, we would stay for a month at a time, it was awesome, but since we got married and had kids, the last couple of times, it's only been for two weeks.'

Right, I thought to myself, so my dark hair, blue eyed, broad shouldered Aussie surfer, was a married Aussie surfer. I felt my body stiffen a little, even though I was enjoying this playful exchange and I really wanted to continue. In the past, I had shamefully not concerned myself as to whether a man was married or not, in my selfishness to get a hit of whatever he could offer me. I was certainly never after any sort of emotional connection. But now I absolutely did care that this man was married and even flirting with him felt wrong.

'Oh, no! I'm not married anymore. I'm staying on longer, alone this time. My wife left me six months ago for someone else. Some guy she works with and had apparently fallen in love with while on a work conference. You know it can happen just like that apparently,' He mocked, shook his head and took another drink of his beer.

I didn't engage, because I wasn't sure if I was just being

told a story to string me along. Again, I was so use to my radar being able to read men, and to quickly determine if there was anything in it for me. But with that radar having been dismantled along with my harsh and selfish behaviours, I could not tell if he was genuine or not.

I picked up my drink, no longer comfortable with my unease. Now that I couldn't feel the playfulness and determine whether it was genuine or not, I just didn't feel a need to continue the conversation.

'I'm sorry,' he said noticing my unease. 'Sorry to go there. It's still raw and I have had a tough time dealing with it all. This break is meant to be my escape to try and get my head together, I should, for my son. He's only two and he needs me. The other guy, he's, well, he stole my wife and I hate him being around him and living with him. I hate not seeing him for this long, but I wasn't really coping too well. I know it is best that I take this time now, so that I can do the right thing by him as he gets older. My wife, sorry, ex-wife will try and use this against me in the custody hearing, but that's the risk I have to take, because I would be nothing to my little mate, if I continued on the way I was. The way I have been.'

Again, he paused and took another drink of his beer. Although he was talking to me, it was like he was talking to himself, in his own pain and my heart felt for him. Touching the side of his arm to get his attention I looked into his eyes.

'Hey I get it. That's why I'm here as well. I totally get it and it's a pretty magic place to heal.'

He softened out of his pain, and smiled.

'I guess when I saw you on the beach, I could feel your pain, and that's why I wanted to check you were okay. I know sometimes, when you're in pain, you don't know in yourself if you are okay and it's nice to know that someone's looking out for you.'

'Thank you,' I smiled genuinely touched by his concern. 'I am good actually, even though this afternoon was all sorts of ugly, it was beautifully ugly.'

He smiled, but there was sadness in his smile.

'Is it working for you? Being away here, is it helping?' I asked, feeling genuinely concerned for his wellbeing now.

'Yeah, it is sort of. Being with my mates is great. I guess a great distraction from my thoughts. We have a laugh and talk mindless nonsense, which is what we do and have always done. And there is comfort in that. The simplicity and familiarity of the friendships. And being in the ocean. That is where I find my peace. Everything feels okay when I am sitting out-the-back, I can just be there and nothing else kind of gets in. And then when I jump on those waves, it lifts me and takes me somewhere else. It is such a ride. I get to feel this surge of power within me and I want to ride it forever and hold onto that feeling. But the wave always ends, then reality hits home again and all my thoughts come flooding back. I paddle back out as quick as I can, to find that peace hanging out the back again. My mates say I'm worse than a grommet, who has just found surfing and cannot get enough of it. And I guess that's true, I'm in the water here, all day, from daybreak to sunset! And it's a bit like a drug, I just keep wanting more. So that I don't have to face my thoughts.' He snapped out of it shaking his head and laughing at the situation. 'It is all sorts of fucked up, and I cannot believe I am standing here telling you all this. This gorgeous woman, who I randomly bump into twice in a few hours, and should be trying to impress, but instead I'm spilling my sob story and admitting stuff that I haven't even admitted to myself.'

I really loved his vulnerability. He was like a wounded lamb and I wanted to tend to him. I wanted to make sure that he was okay. Now, that again, was so not me, in the past it really was all about me, except with Christopher, but he never needed me to look after him. He was so strong and had it *all* together. He probably saw me in the same way as I was seeing this broken-hearted Aussie surfer, as a lamb that he needed to rescue and nurture.

Gee, he must feel like a huge failure then, I thought. I really must call Christopher and tell him I am fine and it was not his fault, he didn't fail me. I was not his to fail, it was all mine and I had to learn it in my own way and in my own time. As ugly as that proved to be.

I wiped a stray single tear from my cheek and looked up to see my wounded lamb looking at me intently. I'm not sure how long, I had been in my own head. It really was a bit of a problem, this disconnecting from the reality around me, while I processed emotions as they came up, and so much came up these days, as I had finally trained myself not to suppress it all. As thoughts came up, I would work them through, even though that meant at times, I zoned out from where I was and who I was with.

'Sorry about that. I just get caught in my head sometimes.'

'That's okay. I know the feeling. Can totally relate. What's your story? Why are you here?'

'An aunties birthday, and my cousins and I just came for a drink afterwards.'

I was deflecting the question, which I really didn't want to answer. At the same time, I noticed that my cousins had in fact left, without saying goodbye. I checked my phone and there was a message from her saying: Cute. Go for it. Didn't want to interrupt. Nite. Take care. Love U. x A.

Oh God. They think I'm trying to pick up. Am I? I turned back to him, and he was again intently looking at me smirking with his eyebrows raised.

'No, not why you're here tonight. Why you're here? Because you're not a local. We've got to know the locals over the years and trust me, I would have noticed you,' he flirted and asked the question, again. 'So why are you here?'

I shook my head, 'Arrgh, you really don't want to know. It is too long and messy to go into. Yeah, but I'm here much like you, to sort myself out.'

'How's it going?'

'It's getting there. I'm getting there. Figuring out me and who I am now. Who I am becoming. What about you?'

'To be honest, until the boys leave, I don't think I'll really let myself go too far into that space. They are all going home on the weekend and I'm staying on for another two weeks. I think once I have that space then I will start to work stuff out. For now, I'm just enjoying the surf and my time with my mates and just distracting myself from reality I guess!'

'Yeah, I know that feeling. I think I did it for most of my life and it didn't really work out too well for me. I've learnt over the last few months that unless you do your work, your stuff is always going to hang around and impact on your life in some way or another, until you face it.'

'I know, I'm just not too sure where to start to be honest. I knew that I needed space from it all. And, now I have that, I'm telling myself that I just need the space from the boys. But when they leave, I'm a bit worried that I'm going to distract myself in some other way.'

'Well, let me help you,' I offered.

He raised his eyebrows and again gave that sly grin. 'You're offering to be my distraction?'

'No!' I exclaimed laughing and playfully hitting him on the shoulder. 'I'm offering to help you get started. I know how it feels to have no clue where to begin. Trust me, I was there only a few months ago. Now I know people who might be able to help you with some alternative healing therapies, that are really amazing and life changing.'

'Well I didn't really want life changing, but that is what I am in the middle of right now—a totally unwanted change in my life and I have to get used to it—I don't really have a choice. I have to get it together for my little mate and get on with my life, so I can make it a great life for him.'

'Perfect! I think this will be perfect for you, once

your friends go you can start doing yoga with me every morning!'

'I love yoga. I'd love that.'

His eyes looked deeply into mine and I felt a sudden tension between us. I know he felt it too, because he flinched slightly and then gulped, still holding my gaze. Here I was convincing myself, that I'd just met this guy because I was in some way supposed to help him, but I couldn't ignore this crazy energy that just seemed to drop itself onto us. Something in me suddenly didn't see a vulnerable lamb that needed saving. I saw a man and all I wanted to do was grab him and rip his shirt off.

'Okay then,' he laughed taking a deep breath, 'what the hell was that?'

Grateful for the break in the intensity of the moment, I laughed as well and shook my head.

'Yeah that, I don't know. But …' I paused, biting my lip contemplating what I was about to do next, before saying, 'I kind of think I want to find out.'

'Well I didn't see that coming, but I kind of want to find out too.'

THE RESCUER

Creeping into my father's home as the dawn broke, felt incredibly *sixteen* of me. I was mortified at the thought of getting caught by my father and was particularly sensitive to him being disappointed in me. For some reason, it seemed really important. I made it to my bedroom and curled into bed. Welcoming the sleep that quickly descended on me.

My precious morning ritual was abandoned as I convinced myself the need for sleep was far greater. I woke a few hours later, to quickly shower, dress and run downstairs to grab a piece of fruit on my way out the door. I did not want to let the children down, nor those that I had been working with the last few months.

My father was sitting on the porch, as he always

did of a morning. He turned as I came out the door and smiled.

'I missed you this morning. Late night?'

'Yeah, sorry if I woke you coming in,' I was embarrassed by his knowledge of my seeming indiscretion. 'I have to run or I'll be late. I'll see you this evening.'

He nodded as I pecked him on the cheek, and ran out the front gate.

When I finished work, I went down to the beach. Which wasn't unusual, as I had been spending most afternoons at the beach, but the difference was, I would be spending time working on me. Meditating, journaling, grounding, breathing. But this afternoon, I was not there for me. I was there to see a boy. A boy who had got into my head and in some respect, was a welcome distraction from myself. I was sick of myself. I was sick of working on my stuff. I know it was important but it seemed like a never-ending task: Was I ever going to get there? You know, where I felt amazing about myself? It certainly didn't feel like it. I absolutely felt so much better than I did when I first arrived here, but that would not be hard given I was at my lowest of lows. Of course, I was in a better place than then. I just didn't feel I was there yet and it felt a little like a piece of string. When was it going to end? How much longer was I going to have to do my work before I felt that sense of true peace and calm within me. And that buzz about life. That energy that just buzzes through you and takes you to that almost euphoric place. When was I going to find that?

Naively I convinced myself, maybe I had found it. Maybe I had done enough work to be rewarded. I had found that buzz again last night, as I lay entwined in the body of this man. This lost Aussie surfer. And I wanted more of it. I had held onto the giddy remnants of it all day, and I wanted more. Just thinking about him, gave a shiver of excitement in my stomach. I wanted to feel him again. I wanted the feel of him feeling me again.

I sat on the beach, not in my own space. I sat with thoughts of him and him alone. I convinced myself I was helping him to heal and in return he was helping me to heal. It was a perfect gift from the universe, to help us both in our healing. It's interesting how we can convince ourselves if we really want to believe something. Truth be told, he was a perfect distraction for me. A distraction from my own work. The work that really seemed just too much without Tabitha around to support me. The work that felt like a never-ending assignment.

The pattern continued for the next week, I would spend all my free time either with him or watching him. Once his friends left, he said he was ready to start doing his work, to start healing his stuff, I stepped into teacher mode, intent on helping him to reclaim his life and redefine himself. We started to do yoga together, and I taught him some of the techniques that Tabitha had taught me to release my emotions as they surfaced and we spent time meditating together. All this time, I was not in my yoga or my meditation, for me, I was doing it for him. To teach him. To be with him. His needing me to guide and help him, made me feel amazing. I felt there really was an underlying reason for having met him. I relished in the opportunity to support him in his healing.

However, the truth was, I was a hindrance to his healing as he was to mine. Our yoga practice would often end in intense love making. That blissful centred feeling following a beautiful yoga practice, directed at ravaging each other's bodies instead of using it to fuel our own healing. It became accepted that our meditation sessions would be interrupted by wandering hands and silent exploration of each other's body. Something, strangely erotic, about being in that place of stillness and allowing your body to be stimulated at the same time. It was addictive in its intensity and I was reluctant to let it go. Even though, I was aware on some level that I was not honouring his experience or my own. I wanted it too badly. And so did he.

When Tabitha returned, I was thrilled to have her back. We met at the beach and I filled her in on the story of how I had met this beautiful wounded soul, and how I had been helping him to heal and to redefine himself after his wife had left him. I told her how it was perfect timing for me to share all that I had learnt and how it felt so good to be able to help others. I told her that he needed her help, on that more intense level that I could not offer him. I let Tabitha know that he only had another three days here, but I was sure that she would be able to help him.

Tabitha simply smiled and said, 'Sure I can work

with him. If that is what he wants.'

'Oh, he does. I have told him all about you and he cannot wait to meet you. He is really looking forward to it. And I just know it will be amazing for him.'

'Amazing for him or amazing for you, my sweet?' Tabitha asked.

'Well him of course, you will help him so much,' I answered a little confused by the question.

'Are you sure? Are you sure it's not about you? Are you sure you don't want this more than he does?'

I was both affronted and confused by Tabitha's question.

'I'm not sure what you're getting at.'

'Please do not be upset with me and what I am about to say. But I have seen this happen before. It is not unusual given what you have been going through,' she gently held my hand.

I pulled away, not feeling comfortable where the conversation was going.

Tabitha continued, a little cautiously to start.

'To me, it appears you have been attracted to this guy who you thought needed rescuing. This lost soul. Like attracts like, my sweet.'

I folded my arms, reflecting my further dislike and discomfort with the direction Tabitha was taking.

'You are trying to save him because you see in him, what you see in yourself, hence the attraction. But, you have invested yourself in him. By the sound of it your every waking thought and action over the last week has involved him, and you have neglected yourself and your own work.'

The shame and embarrassment hit me profoundly at the truth of her words. I covered it with anger and I felt my mood darken.

'There is definitely something special about being able to help others. When and if you are truly helping another, it should have nothing to do with you and how you feel about it. If what you are doing is about you and feeling good about yourself, or getting some sort of sense of achievement from it, then your motivation is internally driven and your work with the person is more about you than them. What invariably ends up happening is that your deep longing to feel good, to feel enough gets in the way of the experience for the other person.'

I felt the tears welling in my eyes, humiliated by my naivety. Seeing my distress, Tabitha again reached for my hand, but I shook her off.

'Invariably, you want it more than they do and you cannot want it for them more than they do. It is their experience and they must walk the path that they choose in their own way. You are simply there to guide and support them in their experience. I can say this, my sweet, because I have been here. I have been here many times before I learnt this lesson. It was painful for me, trying to help others who really didn't want my help or those who just weren't ready for my help. I no longer work that way. But it did take me a long time to learn that. I am sorry but it sounds like you have gone into rescue mode, and I know it felt wonderful for you. To help someone else apart from yourself does feel wonderful. It is often a welcome distraction from ourselves, when we are sick to death of our own stuff. However, what you have done in distracting yourself with him, is neglected your own work and taken on his stuff and you are carrying him on his journey,' she paused. 'Does he really want it, or do you? That is what you must ask yourself. Be honest with yourself this time because it looks like you've been lying to yourself for the last week.'

I was affronted by her bluntness. This was not the gentle nurturing soul that I knew Tabitha to be and I sensed her disappointment in me.

'I am not disappointed in you my friend. It is all part of the experience for you. It is but another lesson and is important that you had this experience and that you learn from it.'

I felt embarrassed and confused and I needed space from her and what I perceived to be her superior knowledge of me and my experience. Then the anger took over, as it always did when I felt cornered. I told her that I had to go. I ran to the water and swam out to wear my *distraction* was surfing. Jumping on his board, sitting opposite him, with the gentle rocking of the waves beneath us, I told him all that Tabitha had said about him, about me and about me trying to rescue him and me wanting it more than he did.

Leaning forward he stroked my hair from my face and nodded.

'Yeah, I can see that. I am grateful for how much you care, and I kind of wanted to do it for you because I could see how much it meant to you.'

Again, I felt the humiliation,

'I do love yoga, but I would have much preferred to be on my board surfing or curled up sleeping beside you every morning. I get the whole meditation thing. I totally do and I am totally into it, but with you beside me, I found it completely impossible to switch off. All I could think about was you and your body, wanting it and we saw how that turned out every time,' he laughed. 'Not that I'm complaining.'

I was mortified that I was so blind. I felt like a fraud that everyone could see through.

Not picking up on my unease he continued.

'To be honest, I've probably done my best work this week in the morning when you have been at work and you have helped me in that, because I did use lots of the stuff that you showed me and it has really helped but, when I have been with you, I suppose it has been sort of distracting. A beautiful welcome distraction, that I'm really grateful for, but I can't really get into my stuff when I am with you, no matter, how much you encourage me.'

My lack of insight into the whole situation embarrassed me. I wanted to run and hide, feeling like a complete fool. Here I was thinking I was helping him, when it fact, I was hindering him.

'Hey!' He said gently, tilting my face up to look at his. 'No one has actually cared for me this much in a long time. You wanting this for me, you wanting to help me so much, meant the world to me,' stroking my cheek he grinned. 'So, maybe it wasn't the smartest way for either of us, but what you have given me in caring for me, is the best healing gift of all. You didn't screw up. It's been an awesome learning experience for both of us.'

He leaned forward and kissed me on the forehead. We sat there for ages, talking, sharing our stories, but this time in a different way. More as two people sorting themselves out. Not one teacher and one student. Just two people who had stuff going on, listening to one another. And it was nice to relinquish the role I had inadvertently adopted and just be me. The truth of where I was. Here and now. And suddenly that felt okay. Just being where I was, with my stuff. Maybe there was merit in the whole experience after all.

Saying goodbye to my Aussie surfer, Zane, was not easy. We really did like each other, but we also saw it for what it was. What it had been. Sure, it was not a holiday romance in that corny traditional sense. It had been a moment in time that happened for a reason. We both knew that there would be no point in trying to continue something more. It was not the right time to welcome each other into our lives. Even though it was easy to keep in touch these days, we agreed, that it was more as two people who cared for each other and not two people who are holding onto something, with hopes of one day making more out of it. I liked the way that we could get to that point. Of course, Tabitha was instrumental in that degree of clarity coming through.

I got over my anger with her once I could see the situation for what it was. In some ways, I was proud of myself, for the development in my emotional awareness and my ability to process through emotions as they presented themselves, as opposed to holding onto them and letting them fester. When Tabitha and I had our first session together, once Zane had left, we worked specifically on identifying where that rescue behaviour had come from and we healed it. There was a lesson in the experience and I was determined to learn it.

I learnt that it was important to balance any old beliefs around this need to help and save others, as it would continue to present itself in different ways until I addressed it. Tabitha had not been surprised by my behaviour as she could sense that person in me, from the moment she had met me. She had seen deep within me there was a healer, wanting to help others and it had been suppressed for a long time. And once I had begun to learn the techniques that she had taught me, and develop a stronger connection to my true self, this aspect of my soul awakened again.

As is often the case, I had not known how to appropriately direct this energy, going straight into rescue mode. We identified, that this aspect of myself had been suppressed once Rosie had ended up in the hospital and it became evident that I was not going to be able to help her any longer. I subconsciously shut down a core belief that 'I can help others to heal'.

It made sense. If I couldn't help her then I didn't want any contact with her, when I look back on my childhood, before this time, I was a rescuer in many respects.

I spoke to my father about this in length the night after the session. He totally understood what had happened to me with Zane, and admitted that he could see what was happening. To think others could see what I could not, shamed me, but I also understood now, how powerful my thoughts, particularly my subconscious thoughts are.

Here I was with my old belief of, 'I can help others to heal' being reawakened through all the work that Tabitha had done with me. It was a powerful belief, that attracted me to Zane and created my 'rescuer' type behaviours. With this knowledge, I was gentler with myself when the wave of humiliation hit. I had more compassion for myself, knowing where my behaviours had come from.

My father told me story after story of my childhood, reminding me of who I was, before 'life' and some of the hard realities of life got in, most significantly Rosie passing, and taking me away from who I was. By his account, I most definitely had been a rescuer, always trying to help any person or animal who was sick, injured or struggling in some way. I was forever bringing home lame frogs and birds from my explorations. If a friend was ever hurt at school I was always the one to take them to the sick room and stay with them making sure that they were okay. At home, when my mum was *off*, my father reminded me, that I would make her cups of tea and fuss over her, doing whatever a small child could to make her feel better.

He explained, and I could see the sadness in his eyes that it was with Rosie, I was most intent on helping. From the day she was born, I would fuss over her, making sure that she was okay. If she cried, he would hear me say in a limited vocabulary, 'mumma bubba cry', and I would get her dummy and pop it in her mouth, snuggle her blanket around her and pat her little head ever so gently.

'Your mother and I would laugh at you. This doting little baby, because you were only a baby yourself. Yet even at that age, before you were two, you doted on your sister like no one else. We would say that you were a better parent to her than we were. You read her so well and tended to her with such love and care.'

And then he shook his head, and could not speak for minutes. As the tears dropped onto the table, my instinct was to grab a tissue and comfort him, but interestingly I seemed to know that this was his hurt and he needed to experience his pain. For me to jump in with a tissue and to say, 'it's alright' and try and coax him out of it, was to dishonour his experience. Somehow, in just one treatment with Tabitha, I was so much more aligned with allowing others to experience their own stuff, in their own way, without me jumping in and trying to fix it for them.

I couldn't help but think, *Damn she's good*.

My father looked up from his tear stained face.

'Losing Rosie was obviously traumatic and heart breaking beyond comprehension for a father.' But, he choked. 'I lost both my girls at that time. I lost you as well, Halia, even before Rosie was gone, I felt I had lost you. I could tell that my girl, my divine gentle and caring little girl, had disappeared. The essence of my girl had died. You lost yourself then, my sweetheart, and I was too distracted with Rosie, your mother, work and trying to stay on top of life, to help you. Oh, I am so sorry that I didn't help you through it then. That beautiful caring soul, who instinctively helped everyone, died at that time. And that is obviously what Tabitha found within you today. She was gone for a long time. It's no wonder she came back with such gusto when you found this lost soul of a surfer who needed rescuing. Probably helped that he was good looking, from what I know of him,' Dad laughed trying to lighten the intensity of the conversation.

I loved him so much. This father of mine. With such wisdom interwoven with his own pain. I could now see that he was still working on his own stuff and so much of his experience made sense to me. The fact that he turned up at the bottom of my hospital bed when he did. The fact that I am here while I heal, while I find myself. It all made sense to me now. I was part of his healing. I was here as much for me as I was for him.

As if reading my mind, he looked at me with eyes that combined sadness and a deep love.

'Halia, I thank you. I thank you for being here and helping me. I am allowing you your own experience and I will not get in your way, and in doing so, you are helping me to learn this lesson also. By doing your work, and finding your way back to you—to who you really are—to the soul that was my precious little girl, I thank you for that, as this is allowing me to discover forgiveness for myself within my heart.'

We held each other, knowing that this moment, and all these experiences were powerful and so important in finding our way back home. Strangely in that moment, I was able to feel an intense deep love for not only my father, but also for myself. I had never felt that before. It scared me a little and I liked it at the same time.

OPENING THE
TREASURE CHEST

I once again carried out my morning routines. The early mornings became sacred to me, I found myself creating this space, not because I should, but because I chose too. The love for myself, that had begun to surface, was directing my energy in a different way. In a way, where I knew what I wanted and needed to do for myself and I was choosing to do these things: my meditation, journaling, tapping, private yoga practice, they became an instrumental part of how I chose to live my life.

I took myself into a wonderful place. A place where I was able to continue to explore me, alone. When thoughts came, when the emotions came, when the behaviours manifested from those thoughts and emotions, I was able to distance myself from them and witness them separately from me as I explored them. I could see them differently and release them.

Of course, there were still negative thoughts and emotions and they got in the way sometimes, but never for long, and never without me having the awareness of myself to know it was coming from somewhere else. Somewhere deep inside, on a subconscious or a soul level, and it just needed to be released.

I began to enjoy the process of healing myself. Things would surface and I began to see it as an opportunity to cleanse myself and become more me in the process. I didn't know what the me I was becoming looked like. What she was going to do or who she was going to be and there was an anxiety attached to that, but not enough to scare me into staying where I was. I had released so much of my anger and my pain, that I was able to enjoy life. It wasn't all so serious and confronting.

Tabitha and I, ended up spending less time doing work together and more time hanging out as friends and I got to know her, this beautiful soul, on another level. She was a wise and loving mother—a gentle yet strong intuitive healer—she was a fun and trusted friend that extended beyond the treatment room.

One day, as we hiked through the Ko'olau Mountain, stopping for a break to take in the impressive view over the incredible beaches that had been my home for six months, Tabitha looked at me and said, 'Who is he?'

'What?' I was confused by her question, as I often was. I had made a point of staying away from men since Zane left.

'Oh nothing, sorry,' she shook her head, in that way she did when she was trying to shake off intuitive information, which she would receive randomly.

'What do you mean by who is he?'

I knew enough about Tabitha by now and her intuition to know when there was something in what she had said. It also did not surprise me that it happened to be here that she had this thought seemingly pop into her head. Here, in nature as we sat on a secluded mountain top with nothing but the sound of the wind blowing through the trees and mother nature surrounding us.

'Aargh! I don't know really. I have been getting a sense of something for a while when I am with you, but it is not clear and I cannot shake it. I don't like going there, unless it is clearer to me, because it can be confusing and sometimes overwhelming for the person, if I open a can of worms with some intuitive feel I get. I've been there. I guess I'm a little over-cautious at times. As we sit here, I clearly received the words: *Who is he. Who is he. Who is he.* I don't know anymore; I suppose I was meant to ask you. So, who is he? Have you got yourself another secret Aussie surfer tucked away that I don't know about?'

'No!' I protested.

We sat there in silence, as we often did when we were together, but after a few minutes I began to feel uncomfortable. I felt anxious here and I felt a wave of panic roll over me.   Obviously sensing this, Tabitha reached out and placed her hand on my forearm.

'It's okay. You're okay. Just breath with it.'

I tried to breathe deeply, knowing I had to keep this panic from overwhelming me. I breathed it out, slowly and surely. Tabitha kept her hand on my arm, assisting me to anchor this energy as it passed through me. It felt big, as if a volcano was erupting inside of me. Funny that, as here we sat, perched on the rim of a million-year-old volcano. As the wave of panic dissipated into Mother Earth. I breathed a *sigh* of relief, grateful that the overwhelming fear had dispersed but aware that it had left an opening within me. Something big had opened, and I turned and looked at Tabitha, again feeling both scared and excited at the same time. Scared that this deeply hidden treasure was finally being uncovered and what that meant. Yet, also slightly excited that this deeply hidden treasure was finally being uncovered and what that meant.

'Okay, maybe I have had a secret Aussie tucked away, but he was a skier not a surfer and he has been hidden so deeply within me for such a long time. I have never spoken of it to anyone and I barely allow myself to go there, except when it comes back in my dreams. I don't know where this is going and it sort of scares me. Because whatever it was, this story I mean, it was just so big, so big that I haven't been able to go there, ever. I don't know what this means.'

Smiling she patted my arm and reassured me.

'Trust it will go exactly where it is meant to go. It is obviously the right time for it to show itself. Don't doubt that you are ready for this.'

I nodded, feeling calmer for her wisdom and her innate trusting in the divine timing of all things.

'So, do tell. You do have something for Australian guys,' Tabitha smirked.

I laughed comforted by her light heartedness.

'Apparently so. I'm like a magnet attracted to them. Well, that is what happened with this guy. I kid you not, it was like a magnet and I had absolutely no control over the situation and I was so young, that I suppose I didn't even know how to process it when it did happen, so I just tucked it away. I didn't understand it. To be honest I still don't, but I guess now is the time that I am supposed to understand it.'

Tabitha nodded, and I could tell by the concentrated look on her face, that she had gone into that zone, of tuning into her intuitive self, that will often provide her with additional information as she sits with someone.

'Go on, tell me the whole story.'

I steadied myself, trying to figure out where to start.

'Okay. I was seventeen. I took my mums car up to the mountains. Mum was pretty much a mess all the time back then. I was playing to what everyone wanted me to be. I remember having this overwhelming urge to get away from it all, and to be in nature and go exploring. I loved skiing, it gave me that time in nature, time by myself and it also gave me a rush that I loved, like what

I would get when I was running. I could really push myself physically and every part of my being would just be electrified. Knowing that I needed to get away from everything and recharge, I took myself to the mountains without telling anyone, I just went on a whim.

It was a magical day, I still remember how amazing I felt. I felt my joy and happiness come back. I reconnected out there on the mountains, in the middle of such beauty. I remember feeling completely giddy on life, with an electrified buzz in me. When I finished skiing for the day, I decided to extend my afternoon a little longer, by having a hot chocolate in the bar before I drove home. It was an extra treat, knowing that going home I was going to be in all sorts of trouble for disappearing and taking the car without asking and I suppose just going back into that life. So, I took my buzzing self into the bar, simply intent on ordering a hot chocolate and sitting by the fire and savouring the moment.'

I paused, as I felt the wave of an emotion overcome me. I wasn't sure why this seemed so hard to talk about, and I couldn't figure out what I was feeling.

'It's okay. You're okay. It's just the remembering. The excitement being activated again. I can feel it too. It's intense, go on when you're ready,' Tabitha knowingly, yet cautiously explained.

'Okay. Okay. I went into the bar and as soon as I walked in my attention was drawn straight to him and he turned at the same time and looked straight at me,' tears were coming into my eyes, 'it was so intense. I do remember now. I can feel it and upon seeing him I don't know something changed in me. Something weird came over me. It's so hard to explain. Which is why I never told anyone or ever really thought about it myself. Because it is too hard to put into words what I felt.'

Tabitha nodded, 'I get it. I totally see it and can feel it. Keep going. I am getting a feel for what this was.'

Again, feeling reassured by Tabitha and her seeming confidence that there was some very good reason for me feeling the way I did at the time, gave me confidence to continue.

'Our eyes locked. I couldn't stop myself from going straight over to him. I don't know how old he was, but I know he was much older than me. Anyway, it was just so weird. I couldn't stop myself from going over to him. We held eye contact the whole time. It was like he knew this too, that he couldn't stop himself from pulling me to him.'

I started to shake and my hands became sweaty and I became uncomfortable sitting there.

'Sorry Tab. It's too much. I can feel it all again and it's too much.'

'What do you mean by, it's too much?' Tabitha's eyes were still partially closed and her focus somewhere else.

'Well, it's just I can feel how I felt then and the need to be with him, that complete overwhelming desire to be with him. It's like a desperate crazy aching in my core. I know that sounds stupid, yet, just letting myself think about him properly, I can again feel the ache to be with him. It is like a desire that is so deep and it feels so old. I crave it and I crave him. I want him. I miss him. Oh, I don't know, it all sounds so stupid. It's just that every fibre of my being had to be with him. In contact with him. I can feel it again, now. Just letting myself connect back into thoughts of him, makes me feel that same aching. I don't know who he is and I obviously can't be with him, yet every cell within me is craving him again now. I want to run away from it. I really don't want to talk about it anymore because, the reality of not having that connection to him, or not being able to have that feeling, makes everything else in life seem dulled in comparison. There is not another feeling like it Tabitha.'

And the wave of despair hit me like a tsunami as I realised that my entire dysfunctional life, from that point on, had been about trying to find that feeling again. I was scared, because this life, my life now, even though I was finally getting into a good place, it just seemed so drab, so energetically dull, because there was just no way that anything in my life could get me to that feeling again. And I wanted it so desperately.

I allowed the depression to take over me. I sat for a long time, in silence with the tears of a loss that I didn't even understand rolling down my face. I knew it was not the loss of him. I don't think I ever really wanted him. It was the loss of the feeling. I just knew that in finding it again, in feeling it again that I had reminded myself of what it was like to not have that feeling in my life. It felt empty and dull and bland without it. *I wish I didn't know what it had felt like. I wish I had never met him. I wish my treasure chest with him and this feeling hidden inside had never been opened. If I shut it back down, then I can just get on with life and be okay with how my life plays out.* All these thoughts circled in my head, trying to convince myself that I could silence my truth. Tabitha broke our silence and had read my thoughts.

'Even if you hide it away, it is still in there, my sweet. It is still inside of you and you cannot forget. You know this. Because even though it was hidden away for so long, it was still impacting on your every day. You cannot not know what you already know. You cannot not feel what you have once felt. You cannot pretend that that energy, that emotion, never existed in you, because your energetic body remembers it. You have been subconsciously chasing this feeling that you have tried to forget for years.'

I nodded, knowing it was all true. I felt that all my hard work on healing myself was going to be undone by this. That I would once again start chasing this seemingly elusive inexplicable feeling.

'Tell me what happened next? I need to know the rest of the story, to be able to understand the soul story that was playing out here. That is what this was, Halia, this was a crazy amazing beautiful soul connection, that wiped you off your feet, and him by the sounds of it. I need to know all that happened to put all the pieces together, to help you better understand the story and why this happened. With this awareness, we will be able to work with the energy to balance it, so that it doesn't throw you off your path again. Okay?'

I nodded, knowing what she was saying was true and trusting her once again.

'I promise, there is a reason for this story having played out when and how it did, we just need to explore that and understand, then we can work on balancing your response. You needed me back then honey, maybe it would have all been different. But it was, it is, all perfect, because it is happening now.'

I smiled at her. I loved her so much. She was such a good soul. And I trusted her implicitly.

'Well I guess what happened, was I walked over to him. I remember him touching my face and it felt like electricity shot through my body and I know he felt it too. I could see the look of shock in his eyes. I could also see in his eyes that he was freaked out by this scene that was playing out so randomly, quickly and publically. But he, like me, could not seem to stop himself. And I don't even know if we said anything to each other. I don't think we did. He took my hand and we walked out. With his hand in mine, I felt myself sink into a deep luscious contentment, that was charged with ecstasy. That connection to him, sent my whole system crazy. So, you can imagine what happened when we really connected, if you know what I mean?' I paused and turned to look at her, feeling a wave of intense emotion overcome me once again. 'Oh fuck, Tab. Oh my fucking God. It was incredible.'

I allowed myself to sit with the memories of that night. The memory of being with him. The memory of going to places that I had never been before. And despite my best efforts, had never been able to since. Seeing the picture now, I could almost laugh at how determined, on a subconscious level, I had sought to recapture this feeling, how I had desperately sought to recreate this energy within me. Looking at Tabitha, I shook my head.

'He took me to another place. A place where I felt like I was flying. It was a place beyond here. He took me away from here. He took me there. It was perfect. It was pure ecstasy. It went on and on. I can't explain it more than that. I know that whenever I ran until I retched I was trying to find it. When I was with other men, I was trying to find it, and the closest I got to finding it was when I did *coke*, my good old friend, *Snow*. She almost got me there. But never quite and that use to piss me off. It never lasted long enough. I needed more and more of it to even get to that point of being close. He took me somewhere. Or, together we were able to go to some place, it was incredible and nothing has ever got me back there. To be honest, here, this life, my life after that point has always just seemed so dull in comparison to that moment, to that night. That makes me sad on one level, because I haven't been able to find it again, and I screwed up so badly trying to find it. In some way, I also feel grateful about the situation now, and that's a first, because at least I got to experience what it feels like to be there while I'm here in this life. When I tried to take my life. I was looking for that feeling too. That is the truth and I got sent back. It didn't come to me when I left my body and I was sent back here.' I laughed at the seeming irony of the whole situation.

'It was not the right time for you to go. Honey, you have to find your there, here. I can see it clearly. This whole life lesson is about finding your *there* while you are *here*. And boy, did you call in this lesson early.'

'What do you mean?'

Once again completely confused by Tabitha's unique understanding of life. She has an extraordinary gift, in looking at life experiences and seeing them as the soul experience that they are, while most of the rest of us, are trapped in looking at our experiences through human eyes and only seeing them for the surface picture that they represent. I was blessed to have this soul reader on my team, helping me navigate through this life. But it often meant that she lost me along the way.

'What do I mean?'

Tabitha paused and did her staring off into the distance thing, clearly feeling or hearing or sensing something. After a few seconds, she shook her head.

'I cannot explain it just yet, there is more information that needs to come to me. I can feel that. I don't know what it is yet, but when it comes it will all make sense. My darling friend, I can hopefully make it all make sense to you and then we can work on healing whatever is trapped within it. Let's head back down, I think I need a change of scenery and you need a break. Sometimes it all gets a bit intense. Let's just enjoy the hike back down.'

I welcomed the change, too.

There was something still niggling and I didn't want to explore it. I was a little exhausted by our conversation as it was, and I didn't have it in me emotionally to go digging further at this point.

THE SHAME

We headed back down through the beauty of the mountain. It felt good to move, to move my physical body in a way that got all that stuff that had just come up moving. A big part of me wanted it to move back into the treasure box where it began and where I could pretend that it didn't exist. But, there was a wiser part of me, that knew it was a blessing that it had been unlocked. I just didn't really know what to do with it now. All these emotions, memories and thoughts were spinning around my body. Movement was good and I hoped desperately that by the time we made it down the mountain they would have released and I could just move on, completely free from them.

Obviously, wishful thinking on my part, the further

we got down the mountain, the heavier I felt. I felt a sort of darkness overcome me that didn't feel right and again I started to panic. As we got back to the car, I stopped, I couldn't get in the car, I couldn't bring this with me any further. Whatever this darkness was, I knew that I needed to leave it here.

'Tab, I can't do it. I can't go yet. There's something and I don't know what it is. It hit me as we were coming down the mountain. It's like all that other energy, the memory of that amazing high got wiped out by some sort of heaviness … *ha*!' I smirked seeing the irony in the situation. It wasn't dissimilar to the day after a massive night on coke, where the high is wiped by a darkness that seems to come from nowhere.

'It's okay. I also got more when we were coming down. I need to ask you. What happened next? What happened that next morning? There is something there, right? Something happened?'

I shook my head. Sitting on one of the picnic tables I placed my head in my hands. I felt an overwhelming sense of shame and humiliation and embarrassment come over. Not the sort of giggly embarrassment, the deep shame sort of embarrassment. A shame that sat deep within my soul. A knowing that I had done something wrong. Something bad.

'Sweet, it can't be that bad?' Tabitha said, jumping up beside me and patting my leg, 'it feels like it's the final piece and it showed itself today. Today is the day that it is ready to go. You are ready to let it go.'

Still with my head in my hands, not even sure how I was going to explain it. Taking a deep breath, I just launched into it trusting that whatever came out, was how the final piece to the story was to be told.

'Well at some point that night, we must have fallen asleep. I cannot really remember that bit. It was all out of this world type of thing, so I didn't really have a clue where I was. When I woke up, I was aware of everything. Where I was, what had happened, how amazing it had been. I suppose I was aware of the reality of the situation, that here I was a seventeen-year-old girl in bed with a much older man, who had assured me he was not married, but did I really know? Nope, he could have been anyone, all I knew was that I felt like I knew him better than I knew myself, and I completely trusted myself with him, and I know he felt this too. With this blinding trust in the situation, despite its seeming absurdity, we had surrendered to the begging of our souls and allowed something beyond magical to happen. In my waking thoughts, I guess I let my head get in. My gut, which I had trusted implicitly the night before was saying I should leave, that whatever this was meant to be, was done. I should have walked away, as he lay there, I should have just left and taken the magic experience with me but I didn't listen. My head got in and my seventeen-year-old hormones got in and there was nothing more that I wanted to feel than what I had felt the night before. And it was there, lying next to me. Seemingly there if I wanted more and I did. I think that is what I am most ashamed about because I listened to my head and ignored my inner wisdom. I had trusted innately my instinct the night before when my head was screaming at me that what I was doing was dangerous and irrational and plain stupid. But, I trusted my gut and I got to experience that: whatever that experience was. I was consciously telling that wise voice in my heart to *shut the fuck up*, because I wanted more and shamefully I made sure that I got what I wanted. Even though, he knew too, that we shouldn't go there again. I forced it and I took advantage of the situation and made sure that I got what I wanted. But I didn't. That was the thing. I didn't get what I was craving because it was different, it was completely different. He couldn't hold me in that space again and I couldn't hold myself there without him. I should have listened to my instinct, it was right. We were not meant to go there again. But we did and he let me down and I was so pissed off. Pissed off with him. Pissed off with myself. Pissed off with the whole experience.

I left feeling resentful and angry and hurt on so many levels. Yet with a love and a connection to this man, that was so powerful that it was confusing and completely overwhelming for me. I didn't know how to make sense of any of it and I didn't know how to process these emotions. I think, now I can see it. I can see the truth in the situation. I was mostly annoyed, bitterly annoyed with myself, for not trusting my gut. And ruining what was, what could have been a life changing experience for me. What happened within me that night, not the physical side of the things, but energetically what happened to me. What I was able to access energetically in that experience, could have driven me in a positive way to access that energy within myself and use it for such amazing things. But instead, I destroyed the possibility of that happening, by listening to my head and hormones and not my heart and soul.

I think I have such negative heavy emotions attached to that memory. I'm just feeling so much anger at myself and so much shame and humiliation. I should have known better. And, I did know better yet I didn't listen. I listened when it suited me and I didn't when I didn't like what I was hearing. From then on, I didn't let myself listen to my inner voice. Maybe I felt that I couldn't trust it or. I just don't know.'

I paused feeling confused and overwhelmed and once again exhausted by the intensity of it all.

'Or maybe, you felt like you didn't deserve to have access to it, to this amazing, extraordinary energy that you had discovered, maybe you felt like you deserved to be punished; maybe you have been actively punishing yourself for all these years for not listening. For not trusting. Maybe your actions over the past 10 years have been subconsciously fostering that shame and humiliation that you believed you deserved and in doing so you have been adding layers and layers, thick coated layers of anger, guilt, shame and resentment directed towards yourself!' Tabitha once again found the words for me that I couldn't quite articulate.

I nodded, tears streaming down my face.

'Yep, that is exactly what I have done. For the last ten or more years. Crazy!'

'Darling heart. Don't you think you've punished yourself enough?'

'Yes, I do,' I nodded through my tears.

'Are you ready to forgive yourself for not listening to your inner voice?'

Again, I nodded.

'Do you want to know how it feels to forgive yourself for not listening. For not trusting your 'self' your true self?'

'Yes, I really do because I can't remember what it really feels like to not be feeling this low-level shame and humiliation. It feels like it should be there, no matter what happiness I am feeling, or even how far I have come doing all this work with you, it still feels like it has to be there, to remind me that I really don't deserve to feel completely happy. I really am ready to know how it feels to be unashamedly happy. To be unapologetically happy and fulfilled.'

'Perfect! Let's do this here and now.'

Tabitha closed her eyes and began doing her thing.

'Let's start by setting the intention, that you release the energy of shame, humiliation, guilt, regret, resentment and anger directed towards yourself as it relates to this memory and any other experience, in this life or in any of your life experiences, along all your ancestral lines and through all of group consciousness and across all times and directions of space. Allow these energies to be released and create space for forgiveness, love, acceptance, happiness, pride and resolve with yourself any beliefs around not being worthy or deserving of these positive energies. And now start to feel them releasing and feel the infusion of these other energies in the space that you have created by choosing to release them.'

Tabitha stood with her hand placed on my forearm and her eyes closed, innately going and trusting where her intuition took her, seeing what her intuition showed her, witnessing what was happening within all aspects of my being as she spoke these words. I had become use to her seeming 'on the run' or 'impromptu' healings. I felt my role in these moments was to just breathe and allow it to occur, to get out of the way of the movement in energy that she was stimulating and simply go with it. I had learnt to take my head out of it, and tried not to consciously or cognitively understand what was going on, as it seemed to block the process. I had grown to implicitly trust her and her work, as I felt the difference within me after these experiences. And really, who was I to get in the way? This was all bigger than me anyway. And I couldn't do it by myself. I could do some of it by myself, but not this big stuff, not this deep soul work. I needed Tabitha's intuitive senses to guide me, to ask the right questions, to dig deeply into it, to expose the truths that needed to be exposed. I needed her to guide the release of the energy attached to all these memories, and programs and beliefs, none of which I had conscious awareness of. I was so full of gratitude for her gifts, for her love, for her compassion and for her reassuring belief in me, that I was enough, and that I could come into alignment with who I was. I contemplated all of this, while she simply held my arm and held the space for me, whilst my energetic body integrated these changes and she supported me while I anchored in these changes.

Her presence, in these experiences, was a thing of beauty.

Her connection to my energy body.

Her connection to her inner self.

Her connection to energies beyond her.

It was like watching an angel at work.

Tabitha had no idea of her majesty, her power or her pure beauty and divinity in these moments. In some ways, she was so disconnected from her physical self, whilst she worked, that she had no conscious concept of her own presence. I tried to describe this all to her one day, and she would not hear it, she down played it, saying she was just doing her thing. She laughed it off, with modesty and humility. She is majestic, and powerful, and beautiful, and divine and it was my honour to be the recipient of her gifts.

A SOUL STORY: A TALE OF LOVE AND LOSS

We didn't see each other for a few days after our hike up the mountain. I needed to process all the information, all the emotions that had resurfaced and I needed time to integrate it all. It had been an intense experience for me and I was left feeling so much lighter for the experience. I felt free, on a level and excited that a lot of this story, that had obviously been a driver for many of my actions and behaviours over the years, had been brought to the surface and balanced. It was still there, the story and the memories of it, but the emotions attached to it and the feel around it was suddenly not so intense. It felt like it had lifted and that I could breathe. I enjoyed the feeling, once it all settled. And yet, there remained an unease within me. A sense of being unsettled about something. While I wanted to tell myself that it was all done, that I didn't need to dig further into that story. I knew that it was not quite done. I knew that I couldn't delude myself again by pretending that it was done.

I sat with it. *What was it that still felt uncomfortable? What was hanging around making me feel uneasy?* I realised, that I was confused. I was confused about the why. *Why had this experience happened to me? Why did I meet him? Why did I meet him when I was only seventeen years old? Why did I meet him and it be impossible to be with him? Why did he come into my life then? Why did he come into my life full stop?*

These were the questions circling in my head creating confusion and some fear. Fear, because I didn't understand and if I didn't understand then it could happen again, not with him but perhaps with someone else. I needed to understand the why, once and for all.

I needed Tabitha to once again help me as no matter how hard I tried, in my journaling, in my meditation, in my tapping, in my deep breathing to access the answer, nothing was working. I couldn't get to it and I was adding frustration to my confusion.

'Why?' I messaged Tabitha.

Her reply: 'I knew this was coming, I've got your why. It finally came through last night. Meet at my treatment room at 4 pm? Love you xxx'

My reply: 'Freaking out, desperate to move through

this. I want it done! See you there. Love u too xxx'

Filled with trepidation, yet curiosity and a readiness to understand and heal whatever needed to be healed, I went to Tabitha's little treatment room. It was like a little cave of all things beautiful and it was inviting, soothing and safe. Oh, my gosh, that was the thing I loved about coming here, it was safe. No matter what was going to go down, or would come up, it always felt safe to do it in this space. I felt that energy around me, as I walked in, to what I knew was going to be a big one.

'OK, my darling heart, what have you got for me? Righto, jump onto the table. I need to do a proper session with you to explore and heal this for you.'

It had been a while since I had had a treatment with her. Most of our more recent work together had been done informally, on the beach or on our hikes. But, this felt like it needed to be done here.

'You need to be taken out of the picture completely. Your conscious mind that is. It can tend to get in the way at times. And I need to be working with your subconscious and your soul today.'

I allowed her to go there. And, I allowed myself to go there. I lay on that treatment table, I felt like I was in a cocoon. A cocoon of safety, created for me by Tabitha. I was warm, secure and snug and I was ready to go wherever things were going to go. I knew that Tabitha was quite extraordinary in her ability to read the being, the whole self, a person's soul and their soul history, but what I didn't realise was her ability to open within me, an amazing and extraordinary ability to see and understand my own soul story.

It is hard to explain, because I could not 'see' it all, I was able to 'see' snippets, but what I was able to do, was piece those snippets together, like a jigsaw puzzle, allowing me to understand the story that I was both apart of and witnessing concurrently. A snippet of information would come to me visually and then it would be followed by a knowing of the story attached to that image. And from this collation of information I was able to weave a tapestry, almost.

A tapestry of my soul story, which in a crazy, yet almost humbling way, made sense of my life. Made complete sense of my actions and behaviours. My whole messy life made sense through the tapestry that was woven that day in Tabitha's healing room. And, as my life suddenly made sense, in all I had done, in all I had messed up along the way, I was able to examine with different eyes: eyes that knew and understood the deeper story, the stronger motivation, the driver of my life, my soul's history. With this understanding I looked at myself and my life with such love and compassion. And, oh, how I felt such deep compassion and an unquestionable and unconditional forgiveness for myself. I was a human being, but what I remembered within every cell of my being, was that within the human body—at my very core —I was a soul. A soul who was simply experiencing a life in this body and with that soul, came all that it had ever experienced before: much like a computer, it stores all the 'data', all the information pertaining to all those experiences.

This 'data' is not necessarily active, but when something happens in this life, then certain data, memories, emotions or beliefs, are activated or triggered and in doing so become active in this life. They are then powerful deep influences, on an unconscious level, on the choices we make and the actions we take, our behaviours, emotions and the beliefs we hold.

Our soul experiences so strongly influence our life. And are our greatest teachers, as we will continue to be presented with the same lesson—experience after experience, lifetime after lifetime, until we learn what it is that needs to be learnt—until we heal, whatever it is that needs to be healed. Until whatever is adversely influencing our life, is addressed and the lesson learnt and the healing done. Only then are we able to make choices for this life free from the past.

When life happens, we must learn whatever it is we are meant to learn from the experience and then let go. Forgive ourselves and forgive others, or, as I have seen in this life, these things will come back to be faced again and again.

Within moments of lying on the table, cocooned in Tabitha's loving care, with her hands placed gently on my crown, I saw visions of a life, with the loving and gentle guidance of Tabitha as she alternated holding my crown, touching my third eye, allowing me to see, placing her hand on my throat to assist me to communicate what I saw and holding my feet to ground me when I needed to reconnect with this reality, I was able to see my soul's story. The story of how it all began.

I see two women, they are identical. They are old. They are living alone. Just the two of them. They seem happy. Content with one another. Their life is simple. They have all they need, mostly because they have each other, their life flows and they are full. They have been happy their whole life and they still are: never wanted for anything, content with the simple existence that they have and never wanted for anyone else. They were part of a family, but in many ways, they were separate also. As soon as they were old enough to set up their own home, they did.

Then I see one of them lying on the bed. She is old, very old and she has died. The other one sits beside her, her eyes swollen and red, her heart emptied. She is lost and frightened and doesn't know how to do this life without her sister, her twin. She simply does not have it in her. They had discussed this. They had prepared for this. She reaches to the table beside the bed and takes a glass. It's filled with something black. She looks at it. She kisses her sister's forehead and drinks from the glass, in one motion and then lays by her sister, holding her, waiting to join her. Her body rejects the poisonous liquid. She vomits. She tries to hold it in. She does not want to stay here. She wants to go. But her body will not allow her. Her body violently rejects the poison.

She is angry, angry with her body for wasting the

poison, her lifeline to her sister. And she is scared. She does not know how to decide without her sister, she simply does not know how to be without her. Her body weak, she shuffles from the cottage, her soul's desperation giving her the strength that she needs, to wander in the woods, finding the berries. The berries that she had been told her whole life not to touch, not to eat for they would kill her. And that is what she wanted. She was proud of herself for thinking of them, and collecting them in her basket, she returned to her home and her sister. Once again, she lays beside her sister, holding her as she eats the berries, every one of them, determined to leave no stone unturned this time around. Her stomach in a spasm, her vision blurred and her breathing rasped, as she felt a calmness overcome her, she was not afraid of dying, no, this would bring her peace. She was afraid of living, continuing to live this life feeling like something was missing, like she was not enough alone, she was not enough in herself. There she found her peace. The only place she knew how to be at peace, beside her twin. And, as that image faded and before I had time to wipe the tears from my eyes, a new image came to me.

Our souls had found one another once again. This time as mother and baby. Such a powerful bond of love between mother and her infant child. And with that baby in her arms, the mother felt a sense of completeness, peace and overwhelming joy that she had not experienced before in this life, and yet it felt so familiar, so comfortable. And the baby girl, was so calm, so happy and so content in her mother's arms.

Then, the mother is leaving with the father on a trip and the baby is not even a year old. The mother does not want to leave her baby, but her husband is insistent that the child must remain in the care of the nanny. The mother is heartbroken at leaving her baby, but her obedience was to her husband as was the tradition of the day, which left her with no choice.

The baby is now sick with a fever, so distressed at being separated from her mother for the first time. The nanny is tending to the baby, yet the baby will not settle and is becoming more lethargic and the temperature will not drop. Another older woman is brought in to assist. She is special in some way, she is known as a gifted one, a healer but this is never publically spoken of, for fear of the repercussions this would have on her and those who had sought her help but the nanny was desperate, fearing she was losing the beloved baby.

The older woman baths the infant in cool water and tenderly administered small drops of water combined with crushed onion and garlic. She lays the baby in her crib and places layers of onion over her body to draw away the fever that is ravaging her body. Now she is alone with the baby and she is placing her hands on the babies tiny struggling body to intuitively read whatever has taken hold of her since the mother left her which feels like it is only hours before.

The old lady closes her eyes and she feels into the baby's body and then she pulls her hands away from the child and her face is overcome with fear and a deep concern. The child's heart is broken, without her mother she is not and she cannot be. The soul is waning; the soul is fracturing. The old lady knows that without the soul, this baby would most definitely pass and her fear extends beyond that for the baby. She is fearful for herself. She knows that if the child was to pass under her care, many questions would be asked and the man of the house is a powerful man with no tolerance for the mystics. She instructs for the doctor to be called and hands responsibility for the babies care into his hands, not trusting in herself.

The doctor arrives and listens to her heart, the beats are irregular beats and there is an infection. There is nothing that he can do to assist the baby, she would fight it or not.

The old lady is with the baby through the night, she is holding her, nurturing her, stroking her, comforting her, talking to her, praying for her, knowing she was a poor substitute for the mother she was craving. Yet, she is desperate in the hope that she can convince the baby girls soul to stay and to convince her that she is enough without her mother.

'Don't give up, baby girl, please don't give up. There is so much ahead for you. Don't waste it. Fight on. You can do it. You've got it in you. Please baby don't go. You are enough without your mumma. You can do it. Don't give up baby girl, please don't.'

The words purge from me as I witness her fading

away. I am so sad for this wee little baby who couldn't see how extraordinary she was. Who couldn't see that she really didn't need her mumma at all, how incredibly perfect she was just as she was. I am devastated to my core for the waste of this precious life.

I hold my hand on my heart, and allow the tears to gently roll down my face. Tabitha, allowing me this time to grieve, gently holds the space for me as I grieve for the loss of me and the waste of the life I have lived. I grieved for me and the girl I was who gave up believing she was enough just as she was. I grieved for the woman I was, only nine months ago who gave up on life, just like the baby had given up on life.

But there was a difference this time. This time, my soul was sent back. I was not allowed to go, not yet! I was not allowed to give up on my life again. I had to do it differently this life. I had to heal this story. As I lay on the table, I was open to whatever else I needed to witness, to feel and experience to allow me to heal and to write a different ending to this life's story.

I can see her. I can feel her. She is peaceful and content and calm. She is by a river and there are big grey rocks in the river and along the banks. There are some trees lining the banks and beyond that and surrounding her are mountains, speckled with the similar grey boulders and interspersed with grass and small trees.

It is cold yet she is wearing quite sparse clothes, a loose skirt and a blouse of some sort and a woven jacket. It looks like a farmer's old jacket, but she does not mind, because she is here. Even if she is cold and a little dishevelled. She does not mind because she is free here by the water, the trees, the animals. Here she can breathe. It is her place to come each day where she can just be, just feel okay being her. She will often sit with the wild rabbits and birds beside her, talking to them.

Now, I can feel the sadness come again, like a wave overcoming her and taking away her sense of peace.

She wonders with sadness if this is all there is in this life for her. These stolen moments each day are the only thing she looks forward to. Her mother knows this about her and blindly turns away, allowing her this. This unspoken reprieve from a life within the walls of an old castle that is filled with ritual and historical ancestral constraints. Her sisters willingly played to this game, knowing that their discipline and obedience to the unspoken, yet clearly defined expectations of their father, would be rewarded by marriage to a man of statue.

This game, the girl was reluctant to play, yet she complied to the extent that she knew she must to be respectful to her father and her family name. She knew, and her family knew, her heart and soul were absent in this life. She was in some way forgiven for this because she respectfully complied to the life she had fallen into, and that is why her mother allowed her, her daily reprieve, and turned her father's head.

It was a given that she would never be married off, not 'the little strange one' as she was often referred in the community. And while she did not seek to be married off, she was often overcome by a sense of despair, that this was what her life was to look like for the remainder of it.

But then, she would bring herself back into the moment by taking her boots off and placing her toes in the icy cold stream. And with that sensation, she would let go of her sadness and despair and allow herself to immerse in the calm that would once again fill her soul.

And that is what he saw when he first lay eyes on her. A picture of an ethereal looking being, loose golden hair flowing around her shoulders, a delicate flower with her skirt hitched and bare white feet immersed in the near freezing stream.

He became her everything as she was to him. And their secret daily meetings became her soul purpose for being. As she lay with him for the first time, she knew she had found her way home. She did not care what her father would say, what her father would do, if he was to find her with him, a servant boy. But, he was not a servant boy to her. He was her everything and as she lay beside him, allowing him to gently caress her naked body, she closed her eyes and felt herself become full, become whole under his touch. As he ever so gently entered her, she moaned with a remembering, as the fullness of her being awakened for the first time. She remembered what it felt like to be whole and she melted into the fullness of her being, only brought to her by his being.

As she wiped her tears of pure joy from her eyes, she looked into his and saw her emotions being mirrored in his eyes. He was in this with her, he was feeling this with her. While they both new that the world was to say that they could never be: the nobleman's daughter, albeit the strange one and a 'servant boy' from a neighbouring estate.

He was no boy; he was a man. He knew that his relationship with this most delicate and exquisite of young women would be severely frowned upon by both his master and her father. But he could not stop himself from meeting with her. From the moment, he saw her by the river that day, and his eyes connected with hers, he could not bear to be without her. Their time apart was empty, their stolen hours together were all they lived for, as he made love to her that first time, in the darkness of a cave deep within the mountain range, he knew he would die for her. He had never felt more sure of himself, never clearer, never more knowing than in those moments of intimacy.

I now see her in a room, lying on a bed in a gown, a doctor is examining her. Her mother and father are in the room too. The doctor turns to her parents and tells them that she is in fact, pregnant and that would explain her recurrent fainting episodes. She is shocked as she comprehends what he is saying to her parent, but then she softens with the realisation that he is with her, as she places her hand lovingly on her slightly swollen stomach. Her father turns on her, slapping her face and hurling insults at her. She feels immune to it, for she is connected to him and nothing can take her away from the feeling she has when she is with him.

She is now being beaten by her father, for she is refusing to talk. She will not tell them anything. Who he is or how this happened. To share it with anyone would destroy the sacredness of their union. And so, she stays in silence despite the beatings, the threats, the isolation.

She is not allowed to leave the house, locked in her room. She is told she has brought shame on herself and her family and is to be sent away to have the baby. She doesn't care about leaving her home and her family. She is a stranger to them anyway. They do not know her. They do not understand her. They never did and she knew that they never would, not in the way he knew her, he understood her. She didn't have to say anything for him to just know her thoughts, her dreams, her feelings, her inner most being.

She craved him again. She needed to be with him again. She felt an emptiness that she could only dispel by connecting herself with her baby. She could feel him through the baby that she carried. It was not the same, and it was not quite enough but it was all that she had. It was almost enough, when she allowed herself to really feel her baby it almost got her back to that place: that magical place within herself of being with him.

She connected to him, through her unborn baby. In her forced isolation, she would sit rubbing her slightly rounded stomach, singing and talking to her baby. Loving this baby, their baby, the symbol of their union, their unique love and connection.

She is in a room now. It is cold and sterile and she is

surrounded by nuns in long black habits. She is labouring, she is birthing their baby. Her cries are left lingering. She is not comforted or supported. She deserves this pain, this punishment for what she has done wrong. The harder the delivery, the more welcomed it is by the nuns as a fitting penance for the sins committed in conceiving the child. They are hardened in their duty. Upon the baby boy's birth, they take him away.

She does not realise, her young, fragile body still shocked by the birthing experience. They mercilessly clean her up and she looks for her baby. She asks for her baby. She calls for her baby. She is told there is no baby. The baby is gone.

She stops now aware of what they have done. There is no disbelief, just a heartbreaking awareness of the truth of what they have done to her. What they have all done to her: her mother, her father, the nuns. They have taken him away from her. Her baby was her only connection to him and they've taken him away.

Her screams of pain and rage were heard throughout the convent and beyond. She would not be silenced, not by their requests, not by their threats, not by their beating. She would not be silenced. She could not be silenced. And, then the doctor comes back with a needle. She is silenced. She is numbed. Her eyes are dead, a reflection of her soul. Her soul is dead; she cannot be without him, not again.

She is sitting at a desk in a classroom. She is in a nun's habit. She is older, but not so much. The room is filled with children; she is their teacher. Her face is sullen and hardened. She yells at a child, abusive in her words, bitter in her tone. She walks from her desk with a stick in her hand, and hits the small boys knuckles with the stick. He cries out, so she hits him again, welcoming his pain and distress.

She is bitter. She is cruel. She is empty. She is dead inside. She is nothing without him.

I sob as I lie on the treatment table, unable to contain my heartbreak and pure devastation.

What happened to that beautiful free spirited girl who wandered by the river? Who had she become? Why did she lose herself? Why couldn't she pull herself back out of the darkness?

I couldn't bear to allow myself to see more from this life. I had seen enough; the pain was too familiar.

Tabitha held me as I cried and rocked and moaned and released the pain: the pain of loss. The loss of myself and the loss of the life, wasted in bitterness. I allowed myself to release it fully, all the pain, the sadness, the loss, the waste. It hurt and it was ugly as I ached. I wept. I heaved. I vomited.

'I know you don't have much left in you, but I feel there is one more experience that you must witness.'

Tabitha gently coaxed me when I settled once again. I tried to protest because I was so drained. I just wanted to curl up in bed and sleep, but I trusted Tabitha and if she felt that there was more that I needed now to heal, then I would do it. I had to do it for me and the old lady and the baby and the beautiful young girl, for they were all a part of me, I knew that now. I lay back on the table unsure of where my visions would take me next, but trusting what I needed to see to heal would present itself.

I see a young girl skiing, her face flushed against the icy cold wind. Her eyes sparkle. She is alive as she flies down the mountain on her skis. As she descends the mountain, she feels like she is flying and all her worries, her fears, her anger, her sadness are left behind at the top of the mountain. She feels free. I see her walking into a bar. She is still shining from being on the mountain, her face glowing and her eyes sparkling. She is beautiful and then I see her see him.

'Fuck. Fuck. Fuck. Tab I can't do this! I can't go here.'

I protest already fearful that if I allow myself to go into that space, then everything will be awakened again, that desperate need for more, for him, for that feeling and I don't want to feel it again. It scares me.

'Sweetheart, if you are being taken to these visions, then trust it is important that you witness it again. Allow yourself to see it. Open yourself to what comes through.'

'I don't want to. I don't want to go here again,' I paused while I collected my thoughts to explain. 'It's too painful Tab, I don't want to feel it all again.'

'This time you will be seeing it through different eyes, you will be feeling it as a different person, you will be experiencing it from a place of knowing and understanding yourself and your story so much better. It feels like it is important for you to witness this life again now, with a new perspective and a new love of yourself.'

Reluctantly, I allow myself to go into that space again, trusting Tabitha's wisdom and knowing I am safe under her gentle guidance and healing support whilst in this space.

As she walks closer I can see their eyes connecting and can feel their soul remembering. They have found each other again, so randomly, and it feels like they are home. In the intimacy, as they lay together and the deeper they connect, I can feel her becoming whole, becoming full, like the missing pieces of the puzzle have suddenly all appeared and fallen into place. She is complete. She is enough. I can feel her ecstasy in that moment and can see her physically transform to a state of complete peace. Her being changes and any remnants of strain within her float away as she finds peace in her completeness, her sense of wholeness.

Then she is back in life, her life without him. Her eyes are empty. Her core is aching from a loss that she cannot understand. It all feels so lacking: everything and everyone. Nothing is enough anymore, not without him, not without that feeling.

I see her sitting in her room, dulled by the combination of alcohol and marijuana. An attempt to momentarily dull the emotions that play havoc with her. She is sad and lost and I can feel the intensity of the apparent irrational rage that underlies all that she feels, like a torrent of water running under the surface, that is about to explode at any moment.

It all feels heavy and so confusing, because she doesn't understand why she is feeling any of this. She is lost in this story that she does not know or understand. I want to reach in there and tell her that 'it's okay'. That what you are feeling is okay, it is understandable that you are sad and lost and angry beyond measure, because you have found your souls greatest love, only to lose him once again.

And, then I realise, that she is within me. I hold my heart space, as I feel her within me and I love her deeply. I love her in her vulnerability. I love her in her rage. I love her in her sorrow. For I understand, her and my heart swells with such a deep compassion for her, for me.

I now see her in a toilet cubicle in a nightclub. She's with her beloved friend *Snow*. She has a desperate look in her eyes that quickly subsides when the coke kicks in and then she is bouncing off the walls, the life of the party. I can feel the ecstasy she is experiencing, but also the underlying frustration attached to it, because while it is taking her there, it's not quite taking her *there*. There is a sense of reservation, a reluctant acceptance that this will be as good as it gets.

I want to dive into that dirty nightclub and rip away the filthy hands that are groping her. But I can see that she is actually separate from it, she doesn't care, she is just using him to push her that little bit closer to home. But they are never enough. I can see in her eyes that she is not even there in the moment with this guy. She is gone, on a desperate pursuit to find her way home, to where he took her.

I now see her with Christopher and there is something different—she is alive again, shining, here with him in the moment with real laughter and genuine joy—I can feel her love for him. She really loves him. It is real. At least for a while it was real. Then I see that desperate need for more, a gnawing aching feeling that was always there in the background, subtly unsettling any sense of contentment within her. Maybe this is enough? Maybe it would have to be enough?

I allow the tears to run down my face, as I grieve the loss of my marriage to Christopher once more. It hurts because I am reminded that it was true to begin and he allowed me to find happiness again. I think somewhere my soul must have forgotten all the other stuff and just surrendered to being here with this kind and loving man. Maybe, it was when I allowed him to love me, maybe that is when my soul forgot. My soul may have temporarily forgotten, but it had not healed it.

I see her high once again. Her friend Snow had wormed her way back in. She is laughing, almost mocking Christopher, as he desperately tries to pull her back out of the hole that she is once again slipping into. She has somehow remembered that *he is not enough* for her and she is ruthless and scathing in her treatment of him. Her artificial joy not able to mask her bitterness and hatred of this life and she attempts to destroy him. He, who is only trying to love her. The girl he knows is in there, the girl he only wishes could see herself in the way that he sees her. As the most extraordinary beautiful magnificent woman. She cannot see this. All she sees in life, and in herself is lacking. None of it is enough and with the lacking comes the darkness. Her heart empties and she loses the fight. She's done with trying anymore. The futlity crippling. The emptiness is always there. The darkness is always there. She wants to just go there and takes the easiest way she knows.

I see the needle in her arm and the darkness become light until it fades and then she is back.

I see her lying on the hospital bed. The edge has been taken off everything and there is a feeling of reluctant acceptance that she has to do this now. She cannot go until she sorts this out. I am so familiar with this feeling. It is what I have felt at every step on my healing journey with Tabitha. A reluctant acceptance that this is time to heal my soul and find my way home in the only true way that one can, within myself.

I finally get it. I finally see it. I finally accept it.

I feel so much lighter and almost excited by this opportunity. I have been given back my life and I finally feel grateful for that.

And now I see her lying on a table.

I see her … No, I see me, right now, lying on the table in Tabitha's room with a pen and paper floating in the space above my body as I hear the words: *It is your story now. Write your next chapter.*

I saw my soul stories layered against the backdrop

of my story in this life, and I completely understood the lesson that I was being taught once again in this life. What had begun a long time ago, continued over many lives, in different incarnations and relationships. Child mother. Lovers. Twins. Each time that connection was a thing of beauty, but also a limitation in allowing the most fulfilling life experience for both souls. For with the other they felt complete and without the other they felt incomplete.

By finding this wholeness in one another, they never sought to find wholeness within themselves. Except when they were alone. Except when the other left them in the life and then they would live a life of emptiness, inadequate in finding their true self without the other.

Now, with compassion and forgiveness for myself, I could walk back into my life, with a renewed understanding of myself—my true *self* at her core—and a determination to integrate the learnings from this lesson into my life, so that in my next life perhaps, I won't have to face this lesson again. And yet, if I do, then I trust and I hope, that I remember my learnings, so that the experience may be one of ease and grace.

I was determined I was not going to carry this story any further. This life had to be different. This life was where this story ended. This is where I, the extraordinary being that I am, remembers that I am enough by myself, and this is where I now choose to live my life where I am enough within myself.

THE COCOON

To say my life changed because of meeting Tabitha would be an understatement. My life didn't just change. I changed. The core of who I was changed. Almost, like it realigned with itself. I still do not know exactly what she does. She is a quiet gentle soul who has this incredible gift to place her hands on the body and heal those parts of you that are broken. And every time I leave her I feel a little more fixed, even though I did not know what exactly was broken.

My dad had taught me not to run away and I hadn't, but I got to a point where I couldn't do any more by myself. I didn't realise this at the time. I needed someone to support me. And like the angel that she turned out to be, she appeared at just the right time, divinely guided to me by her little man.

My brokenness was so deep that I could not access it myself and in whatever way she did it, Tabitha was able to dig deeper and find it. Not only find it, but draw it out for me to see, to understand, to experience and then, most importantly to release.

I learnt from Tabitha that it is all just energy. Everything is just energy. And all this stuff we hold onto, is just energy, all these stories that we create subconsciously and consciously we attach ourselves to. The story is not important. It may help us understand on a conscious level what is going on but it is all energy—and, any energy that is creating struggle or disharmony in our life—needs to be released, so that we can become balanced, calm, flow and feel peace. The lack of peace felt on the outside, is truly only a reflection of the lack of peace deep within. Deep within the soul. My soul found peace and with peace in my soul, I was able to start to become whole once again. And as soon as you feel what it is to be whole again, even if it is just in fleeting moments, then you want to find it again and again and hold onto it always. I also came to know that I was more than what was happening in my 'conscious' world, and that this depth within me also needed to be explored, nurtured and nourished.

My healing here in Hawaii, really was only the start.

That awakening to myself, to my true self, was extraordinary and began my quest to find *her* in every moment of my life, to bring her into my life, to be her in my life.

And just like that, I relentlessly pursued my way home. It was like a drug, living in my truth, with that sense of wholeness: being wholly and completely authentic and in truth. It took me to places that I had only been able to access fleetingly with the assistance of my friend Snow. Yet this, whatever this connection was, I could reach that place of ecstasy and pure joy and lightness, all by myself.

It came and went though, and while I would be frustrated, I knew that it was part of the experience. I knew I was learning to become me again and holding that truth, standing in that truth and living in that truth at all times was a piece of work unto itself.

When I meditated I could get there. During my yoga practice I could get there. When I was journaling I could get there. When I was sitting in silence with my feet in the sand I could get there. When I was with my father, I could get there, his presence so complimentary to my quest to be my true self. When I was with Tabitha, I could get there and I always felt I reached another level of 'there' when I worked with her.

But my problem was that I could not get there, in 'normal' life. When I was in the grocery store, when I was cooking or tidying up, when I was around family and the new friends that I had made. I could not hold me, the me who I knew to be my authentic self. She would slip away and that would frustrate me. Because I wanted to be her, at all times. I wanted to be in my truth always.

I consoled myself, knowing that there was no race. That this journey I was on, did not have an end point anyway, and I was proud of who I had become.

I accepted that I had chosen this life to live and it may take time to learn how to hold my truth in every situation I encountered. If my soul had chosen to be a Tibetan Monk sitting on top of a mountain, then I am sure that I would have awakened to this much sooner, without as much struggle and heartache. If all I had to do was meditate and pray and chant all day sitting on a mountain top, then maybe I would be able to hold my truth. However, this was not what I chose and I also came to know that in a way my life here in Hawaii was not real life either. It was like a beautiful secret cocoon for me—a place for me to do my work, to grow, to evolve, to transform—a place to find my wings and I needed to make sure those wings could fly outside of the cocoon. In the real world. I had to make sure, that I could be me, everywhere.

Sadly, it was time to leave here, to test the integrity of me in the real world. After months in my cocoon of Hawaii, where I was loved and nurtured by my father, where my angel Tabitha guided me back home to who I really was, where I got to know my true self once again, and got to experience the beauty and ecstasy of being whole, I knew it was time to leave and test these wings.

And I was determined, I was going to fly.

I couldn't lose her again.

I wouldn't lose her again.

TESTING THE WINGS AND TYING UP THE THREADS

I found myself sitting in my little apartment in New York City once again. Somehow, I had been wise enough in the middle of my relationship with Snow, to invest in this apartment. I may have been reckless in many respects but I was savvy with my money.

Coming back to New York City and all it held, seemed like a crazy decision to others, but I trusted my gut on this one. And my dad and Tabitha both supported me in this choice. Well it wasn't really a choice, it felt like it had to be done. They understood that I needed to place myself back here, where there would be so many triggers. So many temptations. So much history. So many painful memories. So many people who knew my story. And that was the point. What the naysayers, those fearful for me, could not see was that I needed all these things— the triggers, the temptations, the history, the painful memories and the people who knew my *old* story—so that I could use the incredible strength that I had within me, to write my *new* story.

Yes, the integrity of this new version of me would be tested. The resilience of my truth would be challenged. And I knew that this is exactly what I had to do and I also knew that I had it in me to do it.

Was I scared of falling off the wagon as so many feared I would? As I sat in my little apartment I was completely confident that I had this. I was strong. I was ready to write my new story. I decided that working in law, in the way I once did, was not for me. It was a means to an end, a way to use my brain and make money to service the life that I was leading. I was never passionate about my work. I was now a more compassionate, gentler and emotionally aware person and I knew that these aspects of me, combined with my legal experience could assist others in a way that was more in alignment with who I now was. I most certainly was no longer aligned with corporate life and the twelve-plus hour work days. They were not conducive to my self-care routine that I had created doing daily yoga, meditation, gentle exercise, clean eating and journaling, which I knew I needed each day to maintain balance.

I began my research and discovered a non-for-profit organisation who assisted women and children leaving abusive relationships to re-establish their lives. Included in that, they had identified a need for legal support when it came to financial settlements and custody cases. Often the victim of the abuse was in such fear that they walked away with absolutely nothing coupled with the ongoing fear of losing their children, without custody arrangements legally finalised.

I began working four days a week as soon as I arrived back. I wanted to slip straight into life again and I was so passionate about this work, that it didn't really feel like work for me. Financially, I was earning less than a quarter of what I once earnt, but this didn't faze me, as my needs had become so simple. My financial settlement from my divorce had come through. Ironically the ugly pre-nuptial agreement that Christopher's mother was insistent on, saw me walk away with a sizeable settlement following the sale of an investment apartment on the Upper East Side that Christopher and I had purchased together. I had somehow landed in the perfect position to do this work and still be able to support myself financially.

I relished my role and the fulfilment. I was aware that I could become immersed in it, and it could simply become another way of me creating my enoughness outside of me. So, I ensured that I established clear boundaries for myself when I began this work. This included, working only normal work hours, 9am-5pm for my four days each week, not taking work home with me, not establishing personal relationships with my clients and not volunteering my services on my days off. Many of the other people who worked within the charity, combined their paid employment with voluntary work, but while I was tempted to help on my free day, I was mindful of my tendency to attach myself to someone or something to fill a void in me. I also knew that I needed that extra time to continue my own work. I was not a finished product. I was a better version of me, but there was certainly still work to be done, and more importantly there was a lot of work to be done just to keep my new version of me in alignment.

Being back in my old environment provided plenty of triggers and I knew that I needed to be on my A-Game so-to-speak. I was not going to be pulled out of my truth again. My diligence with, and commitment to, my daily practices was pivotal in keeping me in this space.

I was warmly regarded as some sort of new-age hippy by my colleagues because of my discipline to clean eating, exercise, yoga and meditation. They would gently mock me as they drank their coffee and ate their take-out lunches.

Whilst the courage and confidence flowed powerfully through me, I knew it was the perfect time to heal important relationships. First, I arranged to meet with Christopher, then I flew my mother to town to spend a long weekend here and finally, I invited Christopher's mother to lunch.One might as well jump right in the deep end! Right? I know that I had hurt others and been hurt in each of these relationships. I had already healed my hurt; I did not seek an apology from them because I did not need it. But I did wish to extend an apology to them, for the pain and distress that I had caused them. Whether they chose to forgive me was their choice, but for me I had already forgiven myself and this was in a way just tying up loose ends, important loose ends. How the relationship looked after this was not my focus or my choice, it would be what it would be.

Christopher was wary to begin with. I could tell he had his guard up. He was not sure of my motive in meeting and he was reluctant to relax with me. And that was okay. He had been hurt. I couldn't force him to suddenly forgive me for causing him so much pain. The interesting thing was, as his guard came down a little and we chatted, I could see once again the man that I had fallen in love with. He was still there and I still loved him. I allowed myself to feel the grief of losing him and pushing him away.

It was different this time, the grief that is. I was a witness to it, rather than being in it. I was completely aware of what it was, simply an emotion in response to another. I could see the energy of the grief come and then go. Energy in and energy out, without holding onto what didn't serve me. That had become a motto for my new life. I was not going to collect garbage that held me back and blocked me up.

We talked, we laughed a little, I apologised and he

told me he was still hurt and not ready to forgive me yet. He told me he was seeing someone else and that if my meeting him was an attempt at getting back together then it was not going to happen.

I explained that my motivation was not to get back together with him, it was to come to peace within myself about our relationship. And that was all. I don't think he completely understood, not trusting that I did not have some ulterior motive. I did not need him to understand me, nor trust me, nor forgive me, nor love me. I had worked through this and knew I was enough, I didn't need him to assure me of this. This is not something I could explain to him, but I knew that this process in healing this relationship was part of the solidifying of my enoughness. I felt stronger for the experience and I left Christopher with a loving hug and no need to see him again.

The weekend with my mother was far more challenging, in part because I was not really used to sharing my space with anyone. My time with my father in Hawaii was easy, as he was respectful of my space. But my mother, she was a very different person to my father and a very different energy. There was something erratic and uneasy to her and I felt that I needed to walk on egg shells so that I did not trigger her in some way over some little thing.

She was most uneasy with me when she arrived. I think like Christopher she was suspicious of why I invited her to visit. She was not able to relax, which was very difficult for me to be around, but I had a massive toolkit of strategies to use to keep myself within myself and not affected by her. To cover her nervousness, she talked incessantly about people from my home town, filling me in on all the gossipy news about people I had gone to high school with. Whilst I had no interest in any of this, I respectfully listened and amused myself with stepping out of the conversation and witnessing myself in it. I saw the frustration and irritation building up in me and then gently releasing as I cleverly excused myself to go to the bathroom to rub some acupressure points.

I witnessed my anger rising as my mother began bad mouthing my father, and criticising me for 'racing off with him after he had abandoned me for all those years'. The more negativity she directed at him and me, the more I felt my anger rising. I wanted to yell at her and tell her 'that it was as much her fault as it was his that I was screwed up and that at least he had turned his life around instead of staying stuck in the same rut of bitterness'. But I said none of this, because it did not serve any purpose apart from me releasing anger and attempting to feel better through making her feel worse. The whole, 'I am right and you are wrong' approach. It is so easy to get drawn into those exchanges.

Instead, when I felt the anger was about to explode from me and this tirade of rage spill out onto my mother, I asked Mum if she would like a coffee. She looked at me, quite shocked that I had stepped out of the conversation by changing the focus. I could tell she was shocked that

I had not taken the bait and resorted to my old habits of flying into a screaming raging mess. Calmly, I deeply breathed whilst watching the kettle boil. My anger was like the bubbles of water in that kettle, getting bigger and more aggressive, until they reached that boiling point and then just stopped bubbling and settled into calmness again as the kettle automatically flicked off. I laughed to myself as I silently high-fived myself for being just like the kettle with the automatic off switch.

My weekend with my mother, passed with many interactions like these. Each time I was tempted out of my truth by reacting, I would use a simple strategy to hold myself in my truth and respond, rather than react. Oh, how she triggers me though! It was an exhausting, yet incredibly important experience, for both her and I.

For me, it I felt like I was on a seventy-two hour hold your truth bootcamp. I did it and I was proud of myself for doing it. And I did notice my mother start to relax a little more each day. Sadly, I realised that her unease and nervousness, which irritated me so much, was her response to me. She had learnt to walk on egg shells around me. She never knew when I was going to be triggered and launch into some screaming raging crazy person. For that had been me and that was how she knew me to be. I realised that her constant ramblings about the most insignificant of things, were just her attempts to keep things light. In the past, I would have allowed my irritation and frustration with her to boil over and create such disharmony in our relationship, which would see her walk on egg shells even more. What an unnecessary vicious cycle we had created. And what a gentle cycle we could create, when I remained present with my emotions and gently released them before they took over. The more often I did this, the more my mother could relax, and what I noticed was by our third day together there was an unfamiliar yet pleasant flow between us. Maybe, just maybe I had healed my relationship with Mum, while doing some mindfulness and emotional energy release training at the same time.

And then there was Christopher's mother to contend with. No part of my being wanted to see this woman again. Yet every part of my being knew that it was essential to my healing and in a strange way I was looking forward to the opportunity to test the integrity of my truth. Was I going to be able to hold myself in my truth around this woman? This woman, who quite frankly hated me even before I hurt her son, and triggered the very core of my beliefs around being good enough.

I arranged lunch with Eleanor on my day off, so that I had plenty of time and space before and after to do whatever of my own work I needed to do to prepare for and perhaps, repair from, our meeting. I knew that I would need everything I had in me, and to be in a completely balanced state and my energy body strong and resilient. I really didn't know how vicious her attack on me would be. I was glad I did my pre-work given the onslaught of negativity that she projected at me. I was also pleased with myself for choosing a fancy Upper East Side restaurant for our meeting, as her snobby social etiquette and desperate desire to avoid rocking her standing and not be gossiped about in her Upper East Side social circle meant she kept her tirade to a very polite and socially acceptable tone.

There was no gushing 'welcome home my darling ex-daughter-in-law' going on. She was already seated and steely faced when I arrived, obviously determined to take a power position right from the start. But in knowing Eleanor, I knew that this type of power play would be going on, and I had prepared myself. I was not going to allow myself to be pulled into her game. And I remained consciously aware of staying within my own space, despite the horrible things that she said about me.

Again, I choose to separate myself from the scene and became a witness. It was intriguing in away, to watch my response as Eleanor, spoke so critically of the person I was, all the wrongs I had done to her, Christopher, her family and her reputation. Where once I would have reacted to this attack and tried to defend myself and then be drawn into her negativity, thus disempowering myself, this time, it was like watching a game of Space Invaders. As each attack was directed at me, I would see it coming and then be deflected away, like a bullet ricocheting from an armour.

Once again, I was proud of myself, because that armour was me. My energetic field was clean, strong and resilient to even the most negative of energies. And yet within the armour I was not hard, I remained soft and calm. I was not on edge waiting for the attack and desperately trying to hold my space. I was in the situation and was just me. The new me. The me, who was able to listen and hear everything that Eleanor said, and respond not from anger or fear or a need to be right, but from compassion and love. I could now see Eleanor and who she really was, and she, just like me, was just a soul experiencing life and doing her best. Yes, she has lessons to learn—we all do, and yes—she may not be the best student now, and she may never learn these lessons in this life. And that is also okay. We are all at different stages in our learning. We are all at different points in our growth. And really, who am I to judge?

I own the fact that I had big lessons to learn in this life, and I avoided turning up to class for a long time. I am no better than Eleanor just because I have become more consciously aware of life, my experience in it and my lessons. I am very much still in the lesson and relearning how to live as this version of me.

It was most refreshing to be able to see that we are both perfect exactly where we are at. Not unlike Christopher and my mother, Eleanor was unsure of my motivation, she thought I had intentions of 'getting my hands on even more of the families' money' and referred to me as a 'manipulative gold-digger'. I didn't defend myself, for that was her perception. I allowed her views and her attack, gracefully, holding my space and then I simply explained, 'that I had learnt a lot from my experiences and I understood that I had hurt people along the way, including her and her family, and my only intention was to personally apologise for any pain and hardship I had caused'. Whether Eleanor forgave me or not is inconsequential. That is her choice and whether she holds her bitterness and anger towards me, or not, again is her choice. I knew I had to apologise to those I had hurt along the way. Regardless of how Eleanor, my mother or Christopher feel and whether they choose to forgive me or not, does not stop me forgiving myself. I choose to forgive myself and in doing so I chose to free myself of my past including any guilt, sorrow, regret, grief or need to continue punishing myself. I chose to forgive myself because I had come to a place, where I loved and respected me enough to realise that I deserved the peace and freedom that forgiving myself gifted me.

And so, it is.

WRITING A NEW
CHAPTER: NYC MY WAY

I was six months into my new life in New York City, a simple life that I had carefully carved out to ensure that I maintained my balance and held onto my new version of me, when the Universe decided to shake things up a little. Up to this point, I had been very careful to create my world, my new life in such a way, that it couldn't be shaken up.

I kept my head down and did my work, staying out of trouble and perfecting the art of being *me*. I was playing it safe, hanging around on the edges of life, dipping my toes in, but not allowing myself to get pulled into the deep end where there was a risk that I might drown.

I was being clever. I was being safe. I was toying with life and something or someone decided that it was time I got off the edge and went swimming right in the middle of the pool of life, to see whether I really could hold on in the deep end, where it gets rough and tough. Did I have it in me? I was out in the real world, again, and I was not hiding out in Hawaii. Now, I was living in the melting pot of New York City, there are not many places in the world that are less real than here.

I was fooling myself and the Universe was not fooled. I had been caught out. I had created a mini-cocoon once again in this big old melting pot. Smart yes, on returning into the real world. Essential even. But I had overstayed my hibernation period and I suddenly found myself being pulled from the safety of my newly formed cocoon, by a ridiculously good looking, exquisitely groomed, polished and proper Englishman, with a posh accent and a deeply charming manner. He wasn't my type, he so wasn't what I was looking for because I wasn't looking for anyone, let alone an Englishman, and a real deal sort of Englishman at that.

The moment he walked into the conference room to meet my CEO, our eyes met, I felt the connection and I knew he did too.

Oh fuck, oh fuck, oh fuck. I felt myself start to panic. I knew that feeling. I knew that connection. I knew that pull. It was not just the attraction that goes along with meeting a cute guy, this was a soul connection pull and I knew he had been dropped into my life for a reason, because of the tug at my core. *Oh why, oh why, oh why?* I felt myself being pulled from where I had happily and safely been paddling for the last six months, and with just one look, I felt out of my depth, like I was drowning and I wanted to get out of there as quick as I could.

I knew to trust the intricacies of life and believed in the importance of surrendering to life and what it presented. And with that, I took a massive deep breath to appease my rising panic, and mentally and energetically aligned myself with whatever was to play out before me.

Here goes nothing and maybe everything, except I was determined I was holding onto me this time.

'Hello, Simon Rochester.'

He had an insanely proper Queen's English accent as he extended his hand to shake mine. My breath caught slightly as I shook his hand.

'Hi, I'm Halia, Catherine our CEO, will be here soon, I understand she has just been caught up for a few minutes.'

I was silently hoping she would walk through the door at that moment so this meeting could start and finish and I could return to my cocoon.

'No problem at all, Halia. What a lovely name. May I ask its origin? I've not heard it before, it is quite unique,' he smiled politely, while his eyes danced a little, like he was playing with me.

Nope, not going to play!

'Thank you. It is Hawaiian. My father's family is Hawaiian. Can I get you a tea or coffee?' I asked equally as politely, whilst deflecting attention from me.

'Yes, a black tea, thank you,' he paused and watched as I poured his tea, and his eyes smiled.

'So, may I ask the meaning of your name?'

'It means in memory or remembrance of a loved one, though I'm not sure if my parents choose it because of its meaning. It was just a name that they liked.'

I responded quite bluntly as I didn't want him to continue to focus the conversation on me.

'Yes, well, a charming choice they made,' he again smiled whilst nodding, in some way seeming to acknowledge my wish to diverge the conversation away from me. 'So, do tell me, what is your role in the organisation, Halia?'

I knew I could talk about my work. It wasn't personal. It was just my work. And, I was passionate about it and could happily talk about it all day long, if it kept the vibe that was passing between us on an impersonal level.

'I am the head of the legal team. Well to be honest, there are only three of us in the legal team. There really should be more, as there are so many women out there in crisis who require legal assistance. We are swamped, but I love it. To be able to fight for these women, when they don't have any fight left in them. When they are trapped in the fear of a violent relationship they are fleeing, they really don't know where to turn when it comes to their legal rights. So many are scared to even go there, because they just want to run away from it all and hide. It is important to their future, especially when it comes to the security of their children. Sorting out custody arrangements means they can have at least a minor sense of security around their children's future. Assisting them to process protection orders, divorce papers and financial settlements are vital in setting them up for the future. So many women in these situations are not able to do these things and it really hangs around and burdens them for years ahead. I love that I can assist them in making a clean break with a fresh start by tying up these legal loose ends, so they can move ahead unhindered,' I paused realising that I had rambled and wondered whether I was making any sense and completely boring this man.

He stared at me with admiration.

'You are very passionate about your work, Halia.'

'Well I worked in the legal corporate world for a long time and I didn't have passion in that, so now that I have found something where I know I can make a real difference, I suppose I am passionate about it. I hope I have not bored you.'

'Quite the contrary. This is exactly what I needed to hear. My client, as you may know is a wealthy gentleman who values his philanthropic contributions to society. I assist him by identifying organisations where his financial contributions will make a significant difference to others. While he does make significant contributions to large and well know charitable organisations, he is insistent on finding those smaller charities who are doing valuable work and supporting them in their work, such as *Thrive*. Your sister charity in London is also doing amazing work in helping women fleeing from violent situations and my client has been supporting them for many years now and really sees the value his financial support is making. It is my endeavour to find similar charities throughout the world for my client to support.'

'Gosh, what a great job. To be honest, I hadn't been briefed on the meeting. Catherine and I were supposed to meet just before you came but she didn't make it, obviously, she's caught up with something. I imagine Catherine was planning for me to be involved in sorting out any legal contracts that may need to be formalised, should a relationship be established.'

At that moment, my phone buzzed with a message from Catherine: 'Halia, not going to get there. I'm with Sandra. Maria Frost and son have been found @ new accom. Murdered. Her ex then suicided. Bastard found her. Sandra a mess. Such a tragedy. Internal review of how he found her needed. Please give apologies to Simon.'

'Fuck,' I said quietly, needing to sit down.

I had heard of incidents like this happening, but this was the first time one of my clients had been the victim. I had done some work with Maria Frost but, one of the case managers Sandra, had worked so closely with her and her son for a few months. I simply couldn't imagine her anguish right now. I could feel the huge sense of failure that was welling in my stomach. Somehow, I had failed this woman and her son, somehow our organisation had failed this woman and her son, somehow society had failed this woman and her son. I felt the burden of responsibility and failure descend heavily on me and I placed my head in my hands and breathed deeply knowing I needed to allow myself to feel it but release it at the same time. I'm not sure how long I was in this space, a minute or two, perhaps more. When I looked up, Simon was sitting opposite me, his face full of concern and questions. I had completely forgotten he was here.

'Are you okay?' he asked concerned.

'I am, thank you. I'm sorry I just needed to process some tragic news. Catherine has asked me to apologise as she won't be able to meet with you today,' I continued to explain the situation as best I knew it.

His face went from one of concern to complete distress and he sat motionless momentarily. And then he did the most beautiful thing, he blessed himself with the sign of the cross and prayed.

'May the perpetual light shine upon them, may they Rest in Peace. Amen.'

'Amen.'

I shared in his prayer and stared wondering who the man with the soft heart behind the suit really was? We sat in silence, both processing the situation. He was genuinely affected by the tragic news of a woman and child he did not know. After a few minutes, he stammered.

'Ummm, I think I need a walk and fresh air. Would you care to join me?'

'Yes, that would be perfect. Thank you.'

I quickly grabbed my coat and we headed out into the crisp October air. I didn't enjoy New York winters but

I loved the cleansing feeling of this time of year, when everything was falling away and all the old stuff was being released. It felt cathartic. I needed to be in this space to allow the bubbles of emotions that I could feel building in me to safely and gently release. I could feel myself being triggered and my old stuff wanting to surface, the anger at the injustice, the waste of life, the tragedy of a child being taken so young. I could also feel an intensity coming off my walking companion, that seemed to be growing instead of dissipating in the freshness of the air. For some reason unbeknown to me, I instinctively grabbed his hand and squeezed it tightly, almost protectively. Without saying a word, I was intent on conveying to him, 'that it's okay and I've got you in this'. What I felt was a soul in grief and I knew that I needed to hold him, to anchor him with my touch, to assist him in processing his grief, so great was its intensity. We walked for twenty minutes in silence, hand in hand.

And then, I finally felt it lift from him, whatever *it* was and then he breathed deeply as he stopped abruptly, turned in front of me, took my other hand in his and looked deep into my eyes and said, 'Thank You.'

'It's okay,' I instinctively placed a protective and comforting hand on his cheek as his eyes welled with tears. 'It's okay.'

'I know. Thank you.'

'I have to get back to the office. I am so sorry. I have a couple of big meetings this morning and it feels more important than ever that I fight for these women and their children.' I was reluctant to leave him in his vulnerability, but I knew he had moved through the peak of whatever he was experiencing.

'Yes of course, you must. They are lucky to have you fighting for them. Very lucky.'

'Okay, well, Catherine's assistant, Chloe, will probably be in touch to arrange another meeting. How long are you here?'

'As long as I need to be.'

'Right. Good. Perhaps, I'll see you again in a few days' time. Take care, okay?' I stammered a little as I felt this maternal reluctance to leave him, but knew I had to get back.

'Right, yes. Goodbye, Halia, and thank you again,' he said awkwardly.

As I walked away, he called out to me, 'Halia, would you like to meet later so we can talk, so I can explain this?' Pointing to the tears still welling in his eyes.

'Yeah sure. Meet me out the front about 6.30 pm?'

I felt relief in this invitation because I knew that there was so much more between us that was meant to transpire. I suppose it felt unfinished, whatever our interaction was supposed to be.

'Great. Thank you.' He sounded equally relieved.

SIMON: THE ENIGMATIC ENGLISHMAN

I was completely emotionally exhausted by the time I met Simon that evening. News had spread about Maria and her son, and there were intense emotions amongst the team—anger and rage, despair and disappointment— even a sense of futility. Despite my best intentions and using all the tools I had, I found it increasingly tough to hold my space and not allow the intensity of the emotions within the office affect me.

In one sense, I was a little disappointed in myself, as I had worked so hard at building my emotional and energetic resilience. On the other hand, I honoured the gift of being fully human and allowing myself to experience emotions and to have the empathy to support others in their emotions. While I wanted to be emotionally strong and resilient, I certainly did not want to become cold and closed hearted. To feel love and compassion for others was a gift that I wanted to accept and not fear. I was aware that everything that had happened so far today, was forcing and perhaps gently guiding me to a new lesson, one which I was reluctant to learn, but one which I knew was coming.

Up until this point, in my return to the real world, I had in many ways kept myself quite distant from others and had not allowed myself to really connect with anyone. I convinced myself it was because I didn't really have time for any close relationships given my commitment to my work and my daily self-care practices.

I knew as I walked from the office that evening to meet Simon, that I really needed to align myself with the belief that: I can be enough within myself and experience love and compassion for others.

I had a feeling that the Universe had just delivered my teacher. I could choose to run away from the lesson or I could surrender to what was transpiring here and simply allow.

I was done with running from my lessons, I had done that for way too long, in this life and in so many others. If there was a lesson here to learn, then I was not going to avoid it. I obviously needed to be taken to the next level and this seemed to be how it was going to play out. I chose to surrender. I was not giving up, I was giving in and what was to be, was to be.

When I looked at Simon standing there, I felt a familiar pull again in my heart. It was not love at first sight; it was a feeling of being connected. I know that he felt that too, as confusing as it was, because I could see the flicker in his eye as I approached.

'Hello Halia, has it been a hard day?'

I wondered whether it was that obvious that I was so drained.

'Well, I've definitely had easier days. But then I have definitely had harder as well.'

'Shall we go somewhere for a drink, if you're not too tired, of course?'

'Yeah, that would be nice. Can we walk a little first? I need some fresh air.'

As we walked I told him how the day had preceded from the time I left him and the wide variety of emotions that were being felt throughout the organisation. I explained to him, how it appeared Maria's ex-husband had tracked her location down, due to a filing area in court documentation, which allowed her new address to fall into the hands of his solicitor, who inadvertently had left the file with his client while he went to the bathroom.

Once again, Simon began to tense up the more we discussed the futility of the situation and the innocent loss of two lives. And then suddenly, he stopped and turned to me.

'Halia, I am really sorry, I need to explain. Which is why I asked you to meet me tonight. I felt rather stupid that I reacted the way that I did this morning, and I feel stupid again now, so I simply must explain.'

We sat at a nearby park bench and he continued. 'You see, while I obviously didn't know Maria or her little boy personally, in many ways I do know them, too well, unfortunately.' He paused taking a deep breath. And I sat quietly, allowing him to talk, knowing on some level that this is what I was here for. To allow him to talk, to release whatever it was that he was experiencing. I smiled compassionately at him, encouraging him to continue.

'Oh, where to start, well, to cut a very long and traumatic story short. I was that little boy, but I escaped. My mother did not. And my father did not have the courage to take himself.'

Oh God! This is way more serious than I imagined. This news must have completely brought it all back for him. He must have been in hell for the entire day.

'Yes, it has been one hell of a day for me.'

Had I said that out loud? Or had he just read my mind?

'My father was an extremely wealthy man, he came from old money, so he had never known any different. He was used to getting exactly what he wanted. My mother was about ten years younger than him, she was only nineteen when they first met and he decided then and there that he wanted her. She was incredibly beautiful and he made sure that he did all the right things to get her, wooing her with money, gifts and the pretence he was a good and generous man. When in fact, as I know it now, he was a narcissistic selfish man, who only cared about himself and fulfilling his needs.'

I could feel the hatred spilling out of this gentleman and my heart broke a little for him. It was not in his true nature to be full of hatred, it simply didn't fit.

'He made sure that as soon as he had her where he wanted her, that she stayed there. It was the stereotypical emotional abuse story to begin with: isolating her from her friends and family, and parading her like a prized puppy dog when it suited him. He would pull her in with false love and gifts and then destroy her all over again. I'm not sure exactly how old I was when the abuse turned from emotional to physical, perhaps nine or ten. I don't really recall. My childhood is quite a blur, as you may imagine.'

He stared out into the darkness that had settled. I watched, intrigued by this man who was sharing the most intimate details of his life. I wasn't sure why, except I knew with certainty that I was meant to be beside him and sharing this with him. Turning back to me he smiled gently, a strained and sad smile, one that was holding so many painful memories.

'Thank you. Thank you for listening. I do know I need to talk. It has been a long time since all of this has surfaced for me, and to be honest I thought it was behind me. I have done so much work on it over the years. I truly thought it had healed. But, today rocked my world when I felt it once again, that scared feeling and somehow with you, I don't feel as scared. It feels safe for me to go back into this space, into these memories, into these emotions—I know you aren't judging me, nor pitying me, you are sort of just here for me—and, I am so grateful for that.'

'It's okay, now, what happened next? You need to get this out and now is the time.' I gently coaxed him to continue.

'Well, he started to abuse her physically. All behind closed doors of course, where no one could see and he made sure he kept the façade of happy family going to the outside world, as they do. In all that time, he never laid a hand on me, my mother made sure of that. She would always protect me. And then one day, I think I was around eleven at the time, and I was about to be sent away to boarding school. I suppose I was worried about what was going to happen to my mother when I was not there. Not that I had ever done anything to stop him from hurting her, but maybe I thought that by me being there, it stopped it from being worse that it could have been. I really don't know what I thought. One night, I stepped in and tried to stop him. And my mother tried to stop me, but she couldn't and I fought him. I fought to protect my mother. It enraged him more and he knocked me to the ground, slapping my face so hard that my nose began to bleed and then he kicked me over and over and over again in my stomach and I cradled my head in my arms to protect myself from him. The last thing I recall was my mother's screams for him to stop. I lost consciousness, fortunately alleviating me from witnessing the trauma that he was to then inflict on my beautiful mother.

Who knows what happened next? Only my father and God as his witness will ever truly know the truth of what transpired in those next few minutes. He didn't deny the fact that he had beaten me, but then he claimed that once I was unconscious, my mother attacked him with a knife and in an act of self-defence, he stabbed her. He claims he went into shock and had no recollection of how my mother's throat was slit and her body inflicted with forty-three stab wounds. I wish he had taken me then with her. But he left me there, to be punished, knowing that I would in some way blame myself for her death. Which I did, for many years. By the time, I regained consciousness I was in the back of an ambulance as he had calmly phoned the police to notify them of what had happened: deluded in his self-righteousness, arrogance and sense of entitlement, that he believed that he had done nothing wrong other than defend himself from his 'mentally unwell' wife. Fortunately, my mother was a wise woman and had perhaps foreseeing an incident like this occurring, she had documented all the abuse he had inflicted on her in her own private journals. These were hidden under a floor board in my bedroom, and she had told me that should anything ever happen to her, that I should hand them to the authorities. It was many weeks before the initial shock of the incident subsided. I was hospitalised for three weeks with fractured ribs and a fractured vertebra in my lower back and they heavily medicated me for the trauma.

Then one day, I remembered the journals. At this

stage, my father had not been charged with any crime. Why I am not sure? I think perhaps it came down to the influence his family had within the community that we lived. Money talks and they believed that they could buy their way out of this murky situation. The journals were what the police needed to charge and convict my father for my mother's murder.

I never saw my father again. He died in prison five years ago. And, four years ago I received notification that I, being his only child, was the sole beneficiary of his estate. Included with the letter from his solicitor was a hand-written note from my father simply saying, 'The money is all yours. Please forgive me'. What he didn't realise was I had forgiven him many years before. Thanks to my mother's family, who took me in and gifted me with a semblance of a normal life for my teenage years. I had had years of therapy and over that time, I had come to the know that forgiveness was the only way for me to find peace and freedom from this story and for my life. Unbeknownst to my father, I had already forgiven him many years before. I did it for me, not for him and he did not need to know. So, the very last thing I needed was for my forgiveness to be bought with his dirty money. That is what I saw it as, Halia. It is dirty money and there is a lot of it, an awful lot of it. I had also studied hard and worked hard building my career and I too, had invested my money wisely, with that I had been fortunate to make substantial wealth in my own right. I did not want, nor need his blood-stained money and my forgiveness would not be bought.'

Taking a deep breath, he let go and then he took my hand in his and turned to me, squeezing my hand just a little tighter.

'Thank You. Thank You, Halia, for listening. I have a confession to make. I do not work for a wealthy man looking to invest his money in charities close to his heart. I am the wealthy man who is taking that blood-stained money and investing it in good. There must be some good to come from it, that is why I am so passionate about what I do and the work that you and *Thrive* does. And today, of all the days for me to be here, for this to happen to that woman and her son. I just know that I was meant to be here today, because I had to face all of this again. I know that in facing it all again, I am stronger for it and my passion for what I am doing is only stronger because of it. Yet, I could not have done it without you. When you took my hand as we walked this morning—which in some ways feels like years ago now—you gave me the strength I needed to face it. It was beyond painful sitting with it all again today, as I revisited so many memories and sat with the darkness of it all.

By spending this time with you this evening, it has allowed me to pull myself out of the darkness and I actually feel light, and in that lightness, I feel inspired and motivated to keep moving forward and to do even more, so that my mother's loss and that of Maria and her son and all those others who have lost their lives at the hands of a violent partner will not be in vain. I thank you, again, Halia, for helping me find the light amidst the darkness.'

I was lost for words. 'You are amazing. You are strong and inspiring and I thank you for your kind words, but I didn't do much to help you, only lend you a shoulder and an ear.'

'Yes, I know, you can't see it. Typically, those with such a gift rarely can.'

He swept the hair from my eyes and looked deep within them. Breaking the intensity of the moment, he laughed.

'Are you sure you're not some sort of angel in disguise?'

Welcoming the change in the tone of the moment, I laughed.

'I'm no angel. Just happy to hold the space for you. Now, how about that drink, because I think we both need and deserve it.'

'Sure, thing winged-one.'

Simon winked and laughed as I playfully hit him on the arm.

ALLOWING LOVE

Six months later, I stood in my beloved little apartment, sparse of any of my personal belongings other than my two big suitcases that waited by the door. Here I was, with a healthy mix of excitement and nervousness, which I allowed to flow as I was buoyed by an open heart, full of love for myself and a man, Simon, ready to embark on an adventure: our life together in London.

Two days after our first meeting, Simon finally met with Catherine, *Thrive's* CEO. By this time, he had worked tirelessly on a proposal for Catherine on how the substantial sum of money 'his client' had decided to invest may be distributed. Simon had asked me to allow him to work under the impression that he was working on behalf of his wealthy client, and I of course, respected his decision to work in this way.

Catherine had come to the meeting, as she had with so many others before, expecting to put forward her case as to why *Thrive* needed additional funds, the vision they had for these funds and how gratefully they would accept these funds. Whilst there are many who are most generous with their money, there are many charitable organisations vying for this pool of money. While some organisations have people specifically employed to secure funding, *Thrive* did not have that luxury and that responsibility also fell into Catherine's lap. She was completely surprised and overwhelmed with joy, when Simon indicated that based on what he had briefly seen two days previously and the discussion he had had with me, his client had already agreed to support *Thrive* in its ongoing endeavour to help women and children re-establish their lives after escaping domestic violence.

Later as we left the meeting room, Catherine bubbling with excitement at what had just transpired, squeezed my arm playfully and whispered, 'What did you do, sleep with him or something?'

'No, I think he just arrived on the perfect day to see how important our work is for woman and children. And maybe now Maria and her son's death will not feel so pointless after all.'

Simon's proposal was a $2.1 million dollar a year donation. His client, had agreed to an initial five year contractual period, which included employing more case workers to ease the load on the current case workers, additional security measures for the case workers when conducting home visits, a renovation of the short term crisis accommodation centre run by *Thrive* and the establishment of three education scholarships for children in crisis, that he proposed beset up under the name *The Daniel Frost Education Scholarship*, in memory of Maria's son, Daniel.

I watched Simon, who I scarcely knew, yet knew so intimately in many ways as he had shared his soul with me, and I was awe struck. He was a remarkable man, intent on doing good in the world and making sure his story and his mother's death was not wasted. He was going to make sure that his mother's death counted for something and that young children, who have had their world turned upside down, just like he did, have the opportunity for a great education, so that they can go on and do amazing things in the world, just as he was doing.

I admired and respected him and how he had chosen to live his life from a place of compassion and love, when he so easily could be stuck in a victim mode of resentment, hatred and bitterness. He had chosen forgiveness and was living from love. He combined his passion with a worldly wisdom, business knowledge and acumen to ensure that this money was used most effectively. One of his strong desires was supporting the charity to establish solid business practices and foundations, so that there was room for expansion and growth in the future.

Simon committed himself to working closely with Catherine, for one week, every month to help her take the business of *Thrive* to the next level by creating a strong business foundation. As a result, for one week of every month for the last six months, Simon and I had been able to spend a considerable amount of time together.

I enjoyed this time with Simon, and yet I was determined not to sacrifice what I knew to be important to me, like my yoga classes, my early morning meditation, my journaling, clean food, time and space to myself. I held tightly to my boundaries. I had worked hard to get where I was and I feared losing myself once again. I convinced myself that my deep commitment to, and love for myself, was why I was holding tight to the rituals that I had created. I made sure for the first couple of months, that when I did catch up with Simon after work, it was only for an hour or so.

Although, Simon, had bared his soul to me, the first day we met, I kept most of our conversations about work, which was easy to do, as we were both so very passionate about work. I suppose I regarded him as a close work colleague, despite this yearning to know more about him. I was intrigued by this man. But I knew I was enough without knowing him better.

The week leading up to his third visit, I began to experience quite severe pains in my chest. At first, I thought it was muscle soreness, perhaps I had been a little overzealous with my yoga practice, as I still had that hidden tendency to push myself too hard. I decided to then miss yoga for a couple of days, and whenever I began meditating it would become increasingly sore and so while I tried to meditate, my mind was distracted by, and worried about, the pain in my heart. I tried journaling about it, but my anxiety and fear was all that would reveal itself on paper. I was jamming up, in my connection to myself and I became frustrated, angry and scared.

What was going on in my heart? What was going on with me? Was I losing me? I couldn't lose me? I tried to step away from these thoughts and the avalanche of emotions seemed to suddenly cripple me. I panicked, as none of my go-to techniques that I had become reliant on held me in my space of *enoughness*.

I needed to retreat. I curled on my sofa, overcome by an escalating fear where I needed to be alone. I couldn't do life today. I was scared to do life today when I was like this. I was too vulnerable. I had lost my armour and without it I was petrified to be in the real world. From the seeming safety of my sofa, which felt anything but safe, I messaged Catherine: 'Hey Cat. I won't be in today. Having a few chest pains and not feeling myself. Might need to go to doctor.' I realised as I typed this, that Catherine, my boss, was the closest person to a friend I had in New York now. While I was friendly with everyone I worked with, I had not allowed myself to socialise with them outside of work and while I got along well with some of the people who I regularly did yoga with, it was more of a quick chat after class.

I stared at the walls around me as I held myself tightly in a foetal position, deeply breathing and praying desperately that I didn't die then and there from a heart attack or worse still, that I didn't lose myself again. I was so scared of becoming *her* again that dying from a heart attack was honestly more appealing.

And then I heard the word *fool* enter my consciousness. I breathed deeply, attempting to slow myself down, attempting to calm myself, buoyed by the intuitive voice I had just reconnected with.

I sat up and asked the question. 'Who is the fool?'

You, was all I got. And again, I sat, staring at the walls around me, as I used my breathing to try and connect back to my inner wisdom. And at some point, it hit me, these walls, my life. I was the fool because I had fooled myself. I mistakenly believed I had created a life of freedom, that I was connected to myself, that I was nurturing and nourishing myself, when all I had done was formed another cocoon to live in. I had isolated myself from the real world, by holding on so diligently to my self-care practices. I had been so intent on holding on to my enoughness, that I had worked so hard to find, that I had become cocooned in life and disconnected from the real world. The real world, which involved real connections to real people and not just the Angels and Guides that would come into my meditations and whom I had grown to love. I also knew that I had become dependent on them for a loving connection.

My heart: I felt it flutter and skip a few beats, reminding me that it was there and reminding me that it was not okay, not physically or energetically. Once again, I reacted with fear. And, as the fear came in, my ability to use my breath to calm me, disappeared. At the same time, I almost lost my connection to myself and clarity of thought which was guiding me to a great awareness.

I could feel the last pieces of the puzzle, but with fear ruling, I simply could not access them, so I grabbed my phone and quickly messaged Tabitha, making a silent agreement to myself, that if I had not heard back from her in ten minutes then I would take myself to Emergency.

'Tab. My heart. I'm scared.' I text her and then placed my phone down. I breathed deeply, but I had no control and starting gasping for air and panicking even more. I grabbed at my chest and tears started streaming down my face. My whole being felt like it was on fire and I began sweating profusely. Shaking I curled myself as tightly as I could in a ball, squeezing as far into myself as I possibly could, here, within me, was the only place that I could feel safe.

I realised that is exactly what I had been doing since I had been back out in the real world, holding myself so tightly within myself, that I had become trapped within. Clearly it was not working any longer and the tighter I pulled in, the less safe I felt. I was in the middle of pure vulnerability. Like a tiny sailing boat in the middle of a storm in the middle of the wild Atlantic Ocean. And all I could do was hold on and hope for a miracle.

The miracle came, within moments, although in this it felt like hours. The miracle came in the wise intuitively guided words on the screen of my phone.

'Let him in. Open your heart. You can be enough

and share your life with others. Here if you need to work it through. Skype? You've got this gorgeous one! Don't doubt you! Love You xx Tab.'

Fuck. Fuck. Fuck. I snapped out of my panic attack immediately and felt pure furious rage at myself. *I was a fool. I had fooled myself.* In holding onto my enoughness I had put a barrier around my heart space. I knew, that the severe chest pain and arrhythmias, were simply a reflection of imbalanced, well, not just imbalanced: a completely blocked heart space.

I had been holding onto my enoughness from a place of fear, not from a place of love for myself. Fear of losing myself again and everything that was associated with that. It is intriguing I mused, how fear can morph into whatever you want it to be, while still holding you almost as a captive. Fear lead me to believe that I was in fact, living my new life from a place of self-love, and all my daily rituals were there to further nurture and nourish my being. Yet, the truth was, and I could see it now, all my self-care rituals were driven by fear, that overwhelming fear of failing in this life, that I once believed, or falsely believed, I had failed in so many other lives.

If I *had* learnt this lesson finally in this life, then I appeared clearly intent on not failing it. Now, here when the lesson was being tested back in the real world, I stupidly let fear, fool me into believing that the only way I could hold onto believing I was enough, was to be diligent with my daily rituals which kept me from connecting to others. It kept me from opening my heart to others and truly living this life. Fear had subconsciously got in and had told me two big old lies. First one, I can only be enough if I am diligent with nourishing my soul. The second, I cannot be enough and share my life with others. My beliefs had trapped me in what I can only describe as a false freedom. I thought I had it all together. I thought I had learnt my lesson. I thought I was doing my homework. I thought I was doing everything right. Although, what I was doing was not wrong. Of course, it was not wrong, it was just the energy that was driving it was wrong. Fear was in the driver's seat fooling me.

I was deeply annoyed with myself for allowing it. But I could also see, now with a bewildering calmness that had descended on me, as I processed Tabitha's message, that I was not angry with myself, my ego was angry. My ego had been fooled and its ego was bruised.

'Suck it up and get over it.' I said loudly.

And, I felt my heart opening, like a bottle of champagne popping. With a pop and the excitement of the fizz and then I felt it overflowing. The love and compassion I had for myself suddenly gushed out and I sat and cried both, tears of joy and tears of relief.

I had found my way back, *again*.

I let him in.

This beautiful man, who had gently taught me to open my heart and trust again, was about to collect me from my apartment and we were to start yet another chapter in London, together.

HONOURING THE SHADOW: FACING FEAR TO FIND JOY

'I'm pregnant.' I text Tabitha within moments of seeing those two pink lines on the plastic stick. I know Simon had a right to know before Tabitha, but the beads of sweat on my forehead as I sat on my bathroom floor and the surge of energy that engulfed me as soon as my niggling suspicion that I may be pregnant were confirmed, left me in no doubt that I needed to reach out to Tabitha. I needed help with this.

'That's huge! You OK?' Tabitha responded within moments. She had that innate knack of just knowing when I needed her. I knew that she would be able to tell by reading my message that I was *not* okay, she would have sensed it. She would have sensed my fear and I desperately needed her to help me through. I was self-reliant these days when it came to my healing and growth. She had taught me well. But I didn't think I had this one, not as I noted the intensity of fear that was swamping me in that moment.

'No. Not OK! Can't move. Fear is taking over.' I tried to deeply breathe and reclaim my calm.

My phone vibrated, with that funny little noise that the Facetime call makes. *Oh, that's my girl.* I thought when I saw that it was Tabitha Facetiming straight away.

'Hello my darling. You okay?'

'Hey, my sweet. Nope not good. I'm freaking out here. Totally, I can't move and feel like I'm just holding off a panic attack.'

'Okay, let's just breath then. We know how to do this. Just concentrate on each breath, slowly and deeply coming in. That's it, just like that and holding it there. And slowly breathing it all out. Every bit from the pit of your stomach. Nice. Now go again. Deep, knowing that you've got this. Knowing that it's just energy. And as you breathe it in, you know that you are safely and gently letting all that fear flow from you. Telling it gently, yet firmly, that you've got this and you don't need fear hanging around. Thanks for visiting fear, but don't need you. Don't want you. And release it all. And now just some good clean deep breathes, knowing you're back.

Knowing you've got this. Thankful to fear for showing up and letting you know there's a little something deeper you need to work on. Oh, what would we do without these amazing emotions of ours that are constantly talking to us. Constantly guiding us. Constantly trying to draw our attention to what we need to look at within ourselves.'

And I felt it all, finally lift. My breathing came back to normal, the tightness in my chest eased, my hands relaxed from their tight clenched fist and my jaw, which I didn't even know I was clenching, also released, restoring a sense of calm and peace within me.

'Thank you!' I stared at the screen of the phone, tears streaming down my face. 'What would I do without you?'

'You'd be fine, my sweet. You know you would get through it. You know that. But it's my pleasure to help you because I love you!'

'Yeah, I know and I love you too.'

More tears streamed from my eyes.

'Okay, so now I'm here, let's talk having a baby!'

Tabitha laughed a little at the face I pulled, one of exaggerated confusion.

'Why was there so much fear straight away? What feels so scary about it?'

'Oh, I don't know. Everything!' I knew Tabitha was going to make me dig into this and get to the bottom of why I had such an extreme reaction to finding out I was pregnant. It wasn't that it should have been that huge a shock. I was thirty-three, in a good place in life, I loved my work, I was balanced and happily in a committed loving relationship and we had even gone so far as to have spoken, albeit quite abstractedly, about possibly one day having a baby together. So why was it such a big deal to have it confirmed?

'What's everything?' Tabitha probed more. 'Just let it flow out of you. What makes it feel so scary?'

'Well, I don't know. That I won't be able to do it. Won't be able to be a mum. That I'll screw the baby up. Because I didn't do such a crash hot job of raising myself so what makes me qualified to raise a baby. That I don't know whether I can actually hold it together with a baby to look after. That I'll get overwhelmed and slip back into old ways. That it will change the relationship I have with Simon and it might ruin it and then I would be by myself with a baby and I don't know if I've got it in me.'

'Sure. Good. Keep going, you're not quite there.' Tabitha teased, knowing, sensing I suppose, that the truth hadn't quite revealed itself.

'I don't know. I'm just scared. I guess. Well maybe, I'm freaking out, that if I have this baby, then I will get so attached to it, and love it and then I will lose myself. I will become part of it and it part of me and I will lose me all over again.'

As the tears continued to stream down my face I knew that I had found my truth. I knew where my true fear was coming from and the rest of my fears were stemming from this one big one.

Tabitha nodded for me to continue, knowing that I had found it.

'Okay. Okay, yes that's it. I'm petrified of losing myself again. I just want to run away and cry and scream all at the same time. I am just so scared to have a baby and love a baby and not be able to hold onto me, the me I have worked so fucking hard to find. I see women everyday who I can tell have completely lost themselves in motherhood. They don't know who they are anymore after they have a baby. And I've worked so hard to discover who I am, and every day I do my work to hold onto who I am, and what if I have this baby and I lose that? What if on some deep energetic, soul level, this baby connects to me or I connect to it, like all those past life stories. What if that happens again? What if I lose myself all over again without me even knowing it's happening? What then?'

Tabitha nodded once again acknowledging all that I had said and acknowledging my fears.

'Absolutely, I can see that. Fear is telling you a really good story. It's quickly found a little gap and made its way back in. But can you see how perfect this whole situation is, Halia?'

'It's not feeling so perfect to me!' I managed a half laugh in my struggle.

'The perfection comes in your awareness. Look at how aware you are of how you are feeling. You were immediately aware of the fear when it got in, because you have got yourself to the point of knowing how it feels to be fearless and the feeling of fear wasn't comfortable for you. And you knew it straight away, and your physical body responded accordingly.'

I nodded, understanding what she was saying and opening myself to hearing her fully as I knew there was wisdom in her words.

'The perfection comes in you being so in tune with yourself, that you were able to recognise the fear that had gripped you and work it through to find out where it was really coming from. Sure, you could have convinced yourself that you were scared because you didn't know how to look after a baby and that it might change your relationship with Simon. But the fear would have stayed around, niggling at you and probably creating pure hell for you, if you hadn't had the courage to peel back the layer and face your truth. And look how quickly and easily you were able to do that!'

'Yes, but not very elegantly.'

Finally, I was laughing again and understood where Tabitha was coming from. I had to admit, as soon as I spoke the truth, the truth that I was petrified of losing myself if I had a baby, I immediately felt lighter.

'Forget about whether you did it elegantly or not. What you did was find your truth and you didn't hide from it because that is what lots of people do. They avoid looking at the deep truth because it can be too painful or too confronting for them. So, they dance around the real issue, creating surface issues, that are never really resolved because they are being fed by a deeper soul truth. I see it all the time. It took courage to go digging to find that truth and to face it.'

'It didn't feel courageous; I don't feel like I had a

choice, not with you prodding me along.' After a moment of laughter, I paused as I felt a sense of disappointment wash over me. 'But Tab, I think I found it so quickly because it's so familiar. It's the same story again. The same lesson again, that I am facing. It's an old pattern and I immediately slipped back into that old way of being. I should have known better.'

'It is old, and, yes it was familiar to you. But the fact that you saw it so quickly once again is such a testament to how connected you are to your true self. You could have chosen to not see this for what it really is. Because what it really is, is just another opportunity for you to look deep within yourself and revisit this old version of you. It's what we call our shadow. It is always there and occasionally it will pop up for you to explore again. Some people, who have done a whole lot of work, don't see their shadow when it pops up again, and they let it take over. And they go back into their old ways. They often get uncomfortable again in this space and begin to struggle and then they see it for what it is and do what they need to do, to face it and heal it once again. But what you have done straight away, is felt your shadow, your old 'stuff' resurface and you were aware that it wasn't a comfortable fit. So, my question for you is, what are you going to do now?'

'What am I going to do now? Well, I think I'm going to face this fear. This is not me. These are old thoughts. Thoughts that want to pull me back into the old version of me. The old me, who let fear rule me and make me believe

I was not good enough or strong enough. I've been here before. This all showed up when I first met Simon and I wouldn't let myself get too close. It took me a while then to see it. But this is the same, slightly different story, but the energy and the limiting beliefs are exactly the same. This time I have seen it for what it is straight away. It is an old lesson and I am being asked to revisit it. Call it my shadow, call it the old version of me, call it whatever. That doesn't matter. What matters is, that when I faced this and overcame it that time with Simon, I allowed myself to open my heart and step into a beautiful life. It afforded me the opportunity to share my life with someone, to feel love and to love. And in that I have found a true sense of peace and contentment in my life. I allowed myself to share this life with someone and love them and be loved by them without losing myself. So, I've already done this before and I can do it again. Yes, the connection between me and my baby will be different to the connection I have with Simon and I know I can have a healthy connection with my baby, one in which she is her and I am me. One where we can be together in the most beautiful of ways, yet be our own people at the same time.'

I paused and took a few long deep breaths. Tabitha didn't say anything, but I could feel her support on the other end of the phone. I knew she was holding the space for me while I processed these thoughts, these emotions and the energy, she was good at that.

I took one final big breath and stated, 'I am me and I remain me while loving and nurturing and sharing my life with my baby. I am enough within myself to share my life with my baby and hold onto me.'

'Perfect.' Tabitha laughed down the other end of the phone. 'You are so damn good at this these days. Now you have found that belief, let's just check whether you are actually in alignment with it.'

And so, Tabitha did her thing and helped me to clear whatever was blocking me from being completely in alignment with that statement. And it felt so freeing to shake off that old stuff once again. I did wonder how many more times I would have to face the same lesson, but I guess that was something I would just have to wait and see. I figured I had done well this time. It was intense, it was damn scary and ugly, but it was quick. I saw it. I faced it and with the help of my divine and gifted friend, I could heal it and in doing so I opened my heart to my baby and felt pure joy and ecstasy for the first time in forever.

Simon was thrilled with the news of our baby. Much like having a committed loving relationship, it had never been something that he had really considered much in his life. But it seemed, I was opening him up to some of the beautiful parts to real life. He was so intent on making a difference in the world, that he had forgotten about ensuring he experienced personal fulfilment as well.

He was in awe of me, during those first few weeks because while he was excited about the idea of having a baby, in many respects to him, it was just an idea. I was not overtly pregnant and so it was not real for him at that stage. But for me, the moment I completely released that fear around having my baby, I felt bubbles of excitement, anticipation and love expanding in me. I thought of it as my bubble of joy, because I felt exactly like that, that I was living with pure joy and it was the most magical feeling. Despite the nausea and fatigue during the first trimester, I glowed and could not wipe the smile from my face or from within my soul. It was like I had been injected with a drug and the drug was joy.

I had never been overly maternal but I had the deepest connection to this little being growing within me. I knew and trusted that I had a healthy connection with my baby, I did not fear losing myself at all and my heart just swelled with love for this tiny little person. I was intrigued by her, not that I knew it was a girl, I just felt it and I was fascinated about who she would be and what she would be like and I didn't even fear how I would be as a mother, because I just completely trusted I would be fine. And if I had this bubble of joy around me then, like I had now, then nothing, not the lack of sleep, not the lack of confidence, not the uncertainty of mothering could scare me.

It was the most beautiful experience of my life, carrying my baby, because it took me into another dimension of myself. I came to a realisation one day, as I sat in the beautiful sunshine with my feet on the ground, nursing a cup of tea in one hand and resting my other on my divinely expanding tummy that I had a beautiful connection with Simon and we had created a beautiful life together. I allowed myself to love Simon and be loved by Simon and with him, I was able to nurture and nourish myself, both on the inside and outside. And I was very much in flow with myself and with life. I was doing purposeful work and I was fulfilled and satisfied by my work. Yet, my life, prior to carrying my baby was void of one thing and that was joy. I wasn't miserable, but I was not joyful.

Carrying my precious baby brought me back to the joy in simply being.

FALL. LEARN. GROW.
REPEAT

There on the screen before me, was my baby girl. At twenty weeks, she was a real baby and how I loved her and seeing her there before me, brought a surge of love unlike any I had felt before. I squeezed Simon's hand so tight as I allowed my emotions to flow through me and his eyes filled with tears matching my own. This was our baby, our baby girl.

Yet, in one moment and with one furrowed brow from the sonographer, our world was turned upside down. Those blissful feelings and our baby girl were taken from us, just like that.

There was no heartbeat.

She was there, but she was not there.

My baby girl had left me, yet I could still feel her within me.

What happened next, is a blur for me. Everything that I was shut down and closed off from the world. I went through the motions of the next few days as a shadow of myself. I birthed my baby girl, how, I really don't know, because the strength I needed to do that, I simply did not have within me. And as I held her cradled in my arms and my tears fell onto the tiniest of tiny faces, I felt nothing. I had completely dissociated myself from me. It was too much.

As some sort of survival or protection mechanism, I had energetically drugged myself, creating sedation and dissociation from reality. I was there but I was not there. I was nowhere.

Part of my soul had fractured from the shock and I didn't know or care if it ever returned. I never got to be her mother. I never got the chance to lose me to her. Because I lost her. I lost my baby girl and as a result I lost me, all over again. This time, I didn't care. I couldn't care whether I ever found me again.

Simon was devastated about losing our baby girl, yet it was different for him and he knew it. He was mostly concerned about me as he could see exactly what was happening. He had experienced trauma himself and he knew the importance of being supported in every way possible, as soon as possible, so that I did not slump deeper and deeper into a depression. He dug so deeply into his heart and showered me with love and nurture. He held me for hours at a time, willing me to come back, but I couldn't move. I didn't want to reconnect with Simon or anything or anyone. He never wavered in his love and support of me in those first couple of weeks. He didn't get frustrated or annoyed with me, even though I gave him nothing. He had me, he believed in me and he was not giving up on me.

The crack in my armour appeared when Tabitha walked through the door. Simon had not told me that he was bringing her over. He knew she was the one: the one who had helped save me the last time and brought me back to being me, the woman that he loved. In his wisdom, he knew that if anyone was going to be able to help me come back again, it was Tabitha.

I saw her face and I felt safe. Safe to let my armoured guard down and safe to feel once again. I suppose I had removed myself from the reality and all the emotions involved as a shell of protection, because if I let myself truly be in it and truly feel into the situation, then I did not think that I would be able to cope. That I would not be able to handle that intensity of emotions alone. But with Tabitha, I innately knew that whatever I had to face, I could, with her supporting me.

Tabitha was with me for two weeks, as my friend and as my healer. She helped me move into and through my grief, allowing me to immerse myself in each stage and each emotion. She held that space for me, and of a night, Simon would just hold me, loving and supporting me, as I rebuilt myself. He never wavered, even though he was pushed to the side and must have felt completely inadequate. He knew exactly what Tabitha was doing and that it was exactly what I needed and he knew his role in it, was to just be there and love me through it.

I know that there was so much of losing my baby girl related to losing my little sister, and my association with losing Rosie, was such a destructive one. My only form of protection from ending back on that path, that self-destructive path that I travelled blindly for so many years, was to completely remove myself from the situation that was triggering these associations.

I had Tabitha by my side and she guided me through my grief, my anger, my confusion, my despair, my fear, my guilt, my regrets. She allowed me to spit out my rage at the Universe for testing me, for punishing me, for tricking me. I was furious that I had done everything right, and still the Universe seemed to have thrown the biggest, most painful curve ball to test me, to see if I really had it in me to hold onto me.

I guess I had failed. I certainly felt like I had failed. In the face of what appeared to be the big test. I crumbled. I wasn't able to hold onto who I was when my baby girl was taken from me. I lost myself completely and I felt like a failure. I had failed myself and I had failed my baby girl, she had sacrificed herself so I could prove I had learnt my lesson, and I had failed. I didn't have what it took to hold my truth when it really counted. Or, so I kept telling myself. I sat with these thoughts, in this mindset for days.

Brooding and mulling over it, making me feel completely miserable in the process.

And then finally, I turned a corner. I remember the exact moment, the exact words as I heard them and absorbed them, as they spoke straight to my soul and they hit the right spot I suppose, because I felt myself start moving forward again almost immediately.

It is not how you respond that matters; it is what you do with it that counts. It was true. I was here thinking that I had failed some almighty big test and there was no way back for me, like I only had one chance and I had blown it. Of course, I didn't just have one chance. This was my life and I could do with it whatever I chose. It came down to choice. The choice I made from here was what counted and was the measure of whether I failed or succeeded. I could choose to sit in this story and see myself as a failure and stay in a depressed, withdrawn and with a bitter state of mind, or I could choose to move forward from this experience, stronger and wiser because of it.

I did not want to stay in that negative mindset, because I knew where that mindset may lead me and I had left that life behind and I was not going back there. I was not that person anymore and I was not about to abandon the person that I had become now. Because I know she is a great person, I know she is strong, I know she is living her life purposefully, I know she is more than enough.

It was as simple as that. I made the choice.

And then, I did the work I needed to with Tabitha,

to untie me from any attachments, most of them were just emotions, that were holding me to that story and dragging me back into the person I once was. She was my past, she was my shadow, she was not who I wanted to be. And while she may always be within me to remind me of where I have come from, the same as everything that I have ever experienced is a part of me. I get to choose the part my shadow plays in my life, because this is my life and I am the one writing the story.

INTEGRITY: TO THY SELF BE TRUE

With Tabitha's help I found my way back to me, who I had grown to be. Simon was with me through it all. He was extraordinary in his openness and his understanding of all that Tabitha did with me. He got it. He was such a wise soul himself. He did his own work and dealt with his own grief, in his own way. He had experienced deep grief before and he was able to move through his own sadness at the loss of our baby girl.

At times, I felt afraid of his love for me, because it was so pure and unconditional. I wasn't sure if I could reciprocate it. I shelved this unsettling feeling, knowing it was there and knowing I needed to explore it. I also knew I needed to deal with one thing at a time, and just getting myself back to me and getting back into life was my priority.

In time, we found our flow again. Our life returned to normal, obviously, we were different because of our experience, but we got ourselves back into a normal space. It was what we needed to be able to look forward.

One night, as I lay curled with Simon after making love with him, I snuggled in close and sighed. I felt safe and content. And while I tried to hold onto this feeling, an unease began to rise within me, a discomfort that I couldn't ignore, even though I desperately wanted to. I just wanted to snuggle in closer and accept that this feeling of security and contentment was enough, that my life with Simon was enough.

But the unsettled feeling would not go away and I grew more anxious as I felt it rising to the surface. When I felt, Simon fall asleep, I got up and crept into the bathroom. I sat on the floor staring at the reflection of myself in the full-length mirror. As I looked into my eyes, the window to my soul, I spoke to myself and asked the question that I didn't want to ask, but knew that I must, because it was how I had chosen to live my life, 'Show me truth.'

And as I allowed my truth to come to me. Tears streamed from my eyes, as I felt a deep aching pain, the pain brought to me by truth. A pain that I could choose to ignore because I didn't like what it was telling me, or a pain I could face because I had made a commitment to myself to live my life from a place of truth.

My truth was as simple as this: I loved Simon and he loved me. The love that we shared was so perfect for me, for a period of time. But now, it was not perfect. Time had passed. There was something missing in me, in our beautiful relationship and I had to find it again.

My baby girl had inadvertently reminded me that it had been missing. Before my baby girl had come to me, I had been happy and content and my life was wonderful, just as it is again now. Then and now, I had got myself into a good place in life and in myself, but there was a piece missing in my picture, something that security and contentment could not adequately replace.

It was *joy*. My missing piece was joy. The type of joy that fills your belly with anticipation and bubbles of excitement about what lays ahead and pure joy for what you are experiencing in the moment. That almost giddy feeling of wonderment about what is and what is coming next.

That was missing. And that made me sad.

Sad that I had not been able to find this with Simon.

Sad that I had not been able to find this within myself.

Sad that maybe my baby girl was just sent to me to show me this.

Sad that I had to lose her to see this.

Sad that I knew I was going to have to lose Simon to find this within me.

I curled on the floor in the bathroom, letting the

sadness permeate every cell in my body. I wanted to feel it fully. And then my body heaved as it released from me. Simon found me here. I was curled on the floor, fast asleep from the exhaustion of the emotional release I had experienced. He lifted me and carried me into bed. And as he tucked me in, I looked into his eyes and I know that he knew. I fell into another deep sleep while he went for his early morning run, contemplating what was before us, he aligned himself with what was to be.

His wisdom, his strength, his integrity, his unconditional love and acceptance never ceased to amaze me. It was like he innately knew where I needed to go within myself and he selflessly allowed me to step into my truth.

As he explained it to me when I wondered how he was so okay with my decision to leave.

'If it is your truth, which I know it is, then it is the truth for all. Therefore, it must be my truth as well. I can try and resist it and struggle and create pain and suffering in my life or I can simply accept the truth and move forward. I learnt a long time ago, that fighting it doesn't change anything, only pain and suffering for everyone and I have had enough of that in my life. I love you like I have never loved another. I will always love you. You taught me to live again and not just work and you taught me to love again. Without you coming into my life when you did, I may have never remembered how to really live life and more importantly how to open myself to love again. Of course, I will grieve losing you from being here with me in this way, in this life.

I want you to find the joy within yourself, that I saw our baby girl bring to you. I want you to find it. If you happen then to find your way back to me and it is written for us to be, then it is meant to be. While Tabitha was here, we spent a lot of time together and I learnt so much from her. Maybe she saw this coming, because in some ways I feel like I was preparing myself for this, for allowing this and for acceptance of this. I know that our souls were brought together in this life for so many reasons, and if I look at life in that way, how can I fail to see that our souls are not meant to do this part together. If we try and force something that is not meant to be, then we may well destroy each other and destroy the beauty of what we have created.

I trust, as I know you do. We have chosen to live life authentically and we cannot pick and choose which truths we like and which we don't. We must trust that there is something more at play, and sure we have free will and we could choose to go against our truth, but neither you nor I have chosen to live our life in that way any longer.'

How could I possibly leave this incredible man? The most extraordinary man I had ever met and one that I loved with all my being. It didn't make sense to leave him, but I also knew that I must. For him and for me. My love for him, was the thing in the end that made it easier for me to leave. I knew that if I stayed, I was standing in the way of his truth and changing what was meant to be for him, and I didn't want that for him or for me.

There was obviously something else in life for us, that required us not being together, and I accepted that and allowed myself to leave the love of my life. I was enough without him. I always had been. But that didn't mean I wasn't heartbroken.

I went home to Hawaii, to Dad and Tabitha for a few weeks to heal my breaking heart and ensure that there was enough space between Simon and I, to ensure that we didn't just reverse our choice to be apart and slip back into being together.

If we were done, we were done.

REMEMBERING JOY

If I was going to live in my truth and sacrifice an extraordinary man, I had to define and then find what brought me joy. I had to consider those times in my life when I had experienced pure joy—every memory that I went to, that allowed me to feel a hint of joy involved others or things outside of me—like hiking with Tabitha and most recently carrying my baby girl. They brought me a feeling of joy, but I knew that joy was all reliant on others.

I could not remember what it felt like to feel joy *alone*. In my contemplation, I could not help continually going back to that night: that night in the snow with him, before I needed my 'friend' Snow. I was reluctant to revisit the past, but when I really went searching for my truth and where I experienced joy, nothing compared to that experience. Now, I really didn't know if anything could. Where that took me, where we went together and what I felt in that space, seemed completely unachievable in real life.

Night after night this dream kept coming to me, taking me back to that night. I would feel it all again to the core of my being and I so desperately wanted it again. I knew I was missing something, something that this dream was trying to tell me. And I felt like it was going to continue to tease me, until I found it. I sat in meditation and asked, 'what do I need to know from my dream'. I figured I might as well ask for assistance from some higher power in sorting this one out, because clearly my intellectual mind couldn't quite see.

In my meditation, I was guided to that time in my life, as a seventeen-year-old. I saw myself as a girl trapped within herself, a girl in pain, a girl in grief, a girl in struggle. A girl who had lost herself and her zest for life. A girl who had forgotten how to be herself. A girl who had forgotten how to feel love, for herself, for others, for everything around her, for her life. I saw a girl who carried a deep aching sorrow, for in her infinite wisdom, she knew that it wasn't meant to be like this.

And then I saw a girl, who took a breath one morning and silently said, *No More*. A girl who had the courage to listen to that truth, that it wasn't meant to be this way. And I saw her take the keys to the car and drive. I saw her listening to music as she wound up the snowy mountain.

I felt her whole being become lighter. I saw her flying down the mountain top with complete freedom and flow. Completely at one with nature, completely at one within herself. She did not doubt that next corner that she approached, she just leaned into it and moved where her being guided her.

And, she flowed.

And, in that flow, she found her freedom again.

And, in that freedom, she found her joy again.

And, in that joy, she found herself again.

And, in finding herself again, she found *there* while she was *here*.

She found *home*.

As the tears rolled down my cheek I finally realised that he didn't take me there, I had found my way home all by myself. And, it was when I found home by myself, that I found him again. My whole belief around who I was, changed in that moment when I realised that I hadn't needed him to take me there after all. I knew that if I had done it at seventeen, that I could do it again. I could find my way back there. Everything else that I had experienced in between, was just that: experiences.

Now, it didn't feel scary on my new journey of self-discovery. I felt excited by it as it was just another simple piece of the puzzle needed to be put in place, so that I could find my way, again. Yet, there was one lingering thought, which I couldn't shake as I prepared myself for my next journey into myself. I journaled it, because the answers came so simply when I got out of my head and just wrote: What if I find this piece of the puzzle and the puzzle is still not complete? What happens if I get to the point of living every day in pure joy and I still don't find that feeling, that seemingly elusive feeling of home?

Beautiful girl, get out of your own way. Just tell fear to fuck off. When you are in each moment just breath in the air around you, and cherish that moment and cherish that breath. And let yourself be home. Because that is home.
You are closer than you think!
Find this piece and live in this peace and then your soul might allow you to have your puzzle complete. Life doesn't mess with your puzzle; you mess with your puzzle! Your soul says when it is time, when you are done. It is a choice. It is your choice to continue to keep pushing, striving and forcing your life and your lessons or to choose to stop and award yourself the freedom of saying 'Enough'.
And look what happened, once upon a time, when for just one crazy day you let yourself be completely you, complete freedom, complete flow, complete joy, complete love, complete acceptance, complete trust. Magic Happened. Because you said your puzzle was complete.
Find your joy and live it every day. Listen to your heart and when you are ready to stop. You will stop. Your puzzle will be complete and you will be 'home' again.

I decided to give myself a year and I called it my *year of joy*, and all I was to do in that year, was that which brought me that feeling of joy. It could not be reliant on another. It was mine to find. Maybe, just maybe if I felt it often enough it would have a cumulative effect and maybe, just maybe I might find my way back to that place. The place I only knew as home, and let myself stay there.

THE YEAR OF
LIVING JOYFULLY

I knew that living in New York City and London, was not in alignment with my souls yearning for light and nature, and freedom and flow, even though I loved both cities, they did not support my soul or its quest for joy. Hawaii had allowed me the freedom and flow that I needed and it seemed an obvious choice, but I felt it was done and I wanted something new. Somewhere where nobody knew me, somewhere I could start fresh and not have the possibility of leaning on anyone in my quest for joyful living. It was up to me, to find it within myself. All I needed was a place that allowed me to live a simple life, close to nature, to do some basic work, look after my body and fill my days with the things that brought me joy. To do that I needed to remember what they were. The simpler the life I was living, the less external demand there would be on me, which would allow me to just do what I want.

Of course, I would need to make some money, but I had many skills that enabled me to set myself up on a number of freelancing websites, that enabled me to do copywriting and creative writing work for people. The beauty was, I could pick and choose, which projects I worked on and whom I worked with and how much or how little I worked. I also decided to do my own writing, as that was something that brought me joy. Just sitting in a space, listening to music, sipping on a coffee and not thinking and allowing the words to flow from me. I decided to start my own blog called, *The Year of Living Joyfully* and created an Instagram account to capture moments in time that brought me joy. It became like an old diary that I could scroll through and be taken back to that moment and that feeling at any time. They would be my anchoring tools because I knew that there would be times, when it was more challenging to find that inner joy. If I could look at a photo or read a blog post that took me back to that place in that moment with that feeling, then my body would remember and I would be able to elicit that emotion again, and the switch in me I labelled *joy*, would get flicked on again. This became a key part of my journey and kept me connected to my intention of living my life with joy.

Daily, I was aware of how I was feeling in the moment, and I honoured a commitment to myself, that I would not force a moment or capture an experience, visually or in words, unless it was true joy. I would allow it to flow and become whatever it was meant to be. Planning didn't bring me joy. Being spontaneous did.

And, that is how I found myself living in Bali. I had one bag, my laptop and my phone, I really didn't need anything else. I found a villa to stay in on a week to week basis. It was close to the ocean and away from the general tourist areas, so I felt a greater connection to the real Bali.

It was simple, it was beautiful, the people were incredibly kind and deeply spiritual in their own way and I was drawn to their tradition of offerings. I began my own morning offerings which brought me into a place of gratitude for all that I was, all that I had, for the food that I ate, to the feeling of sun on my face, for all that I had experienced in moments of light and moments of dark and for who I had become. Each day as I offered gratitude, I asked for a day filled with joy and I opened myself further to receiving the abundance of joy. Each day my motto was: I do what I want and I do what brings me joy. I honoured this motto and found a beautiful flow in my days.

It was different to my time in Hawaii, because I wasn't working on my stuff, I wasn't in a healing process. Here, I was just living a life that I wanted to and my 'stuff' was getting taken care of behind the scenes.

I woke early most days to watch the sunrise over

the water; I would wander along the beach, sit and do some writing, for me or for my clients, I would meditate, I would swim, I would do some yoga. I didn't plan it and I didn't stick to one thing. I did what felt right on the day. Sometimes, I wouldn't leave the beach until mid-morning, when the sun would start to get too warm. Time would just float by and I was not concerned, because I had to be nowhere but in that moment and that afforded me the freedom to just be. I loved the feeling of not rushing and having no agenda to follow and being at peace within myself.

I very much enjoyed being alone, but not all the time. I really enjoyed having a connection to others, whether they were the local people or other people on holidays or others like me, who were staying here a little longer.

I met a yoga instructor who was a gorgeous Australian girl named Georgia, who had been living in Bali for many years. She held classes on the beach and in a small studio and by going along to some of her classes I met some wonderful people who were also doing their *thing* in Bali. I knew I wasn't alone in finding my way to this simple island to just be. I enjoyed meeting these people and hanging out with them, often having lunch or dinner together after classes. Everyone had a reason for being here, everyone had a story. I had a reason for being here. I had a story. But I wasn't my story. My story was old and I wasn't attaching myself to it any longer. I didn't share my old story with others. Because every time I shared my story, I energetically attached myself to it again. All those emotions, all those experiences, they energetically brought me back to that place and that time and I was so bored by it.

I had learnt what I needed to learn from it. I had done my work. And I had let it go. I let it go because it didn't bring me joy. I was not my past. I was a product of my past. When people asked what I was doing here in Bali, I told them my story, my now story, which was I was simply here living joyfully. No before. No after. Just now, choosing to do whatever brought me joy and it seemed the simpler my life the better.

Georgia and her partner, who was a semi-professional surfer, also ran a surf school. This part of Bali was known for its great surf and lots of families came here for surfing holidays. I loved the idea of learning to surf, it had been there when I was in Hawaii, but I wasn't in the right space to learn then. Nor would I have appreciated it, in the way I did now. It fitted into my prerequisite for living joyfully. I enjoyed learning. I enjoyed being in the water. And I felt like surfing was going to feel much like snow skiing. I kept getting taken back to how I felt that day when I took myself skiing all those years ago. I was in pure joy as I glided down the mountain, completely at one with wherever the snow took me. Moving with it. Flowing with it. And with so much freedom that I almost felt like I was flying down the mountain. It certainly didn't feel like that to start with. There was no flow. There was lots of laughter and a crazy buzz within me that came with learning something new and the desire to master it. That old aspect of me, that thrived on achieving came rushing back. I had silenced her for so long because I didn't like where she had taken me. But she was me. I didn't need to hide myself from aiming high and achieving, I could work with it, I just needed to do it in a balanced way.

After a few lessons with Georgia, I approached my surfing much like I did my yoga. I practiced it most days. I loved being in that space. I didn't care if I was getting it right or not. I fell off a lot, but I found so much joy in landing in that water after being carried along by a wave. The waves were only small to start with but I still got that feeling of flow every time I caught one and the longer I stayed on one, the more freedom I felt. I kept my surfing in the 'brings me joy' category not the 'I need this hit' category. There was a lot of giggles, a natural high that comes with learning something new and a sense of pride in the mastering of something new. It was balanced. It was freedom and flow. It was simple fun. It was joy. It was a beautiful reflection of the life I was creating here in Bali.

After six months, I had to leave Bali to renew my Social Visa. I had learnt from other ex-pats living in Bali that I could just duck over to Singapore for a couple of days and complete all the paperwork at the Embassy and then I would be able to return and stay another six months on another Social Visa. It sounded simple, and that was my plan, yet as the time approached to go, I wasn't sure that I was going to stay another six months. I loved it here but to be honest it seemed just a little *too* easy here. It was easy to live in joy here, but was here real? These thoughts began to dance around in my head, creating unease and struggle and tempted me out of my joyful bubble.

Does it matter if it isn't real? What is real anyway? This isn't real life. This is just playing. You should go back to the real world and settle down and get a real job. You should never have left Simon. You've had your fun. Now go and live life properly.

I felt physically nauseas at the idea of a real job and settling down. It felt so restrictive and suffocating to me. This little plant thrived in a world of freedom and flow, not constraint and restriction. When I silenced my head and really examined my truth, it was obvious that my life was working for me here. I could earn money, definitely more than enough for me to live on, through my copywriting work, which I was easily able to manage online from anywhere. I had repeat clients and new clients seeking my services all the time. I really enjoyed the variety of work and the flexibility to do it whenever I wanted, or not. It was never a strain and I never allowed it to become a stress for me. It was something that I enjoyed doing and I happened to get paid well for doing something I loved. It allowed me the freedom to do what I wanted to do while here in Bali and to also save enough money to travel more, if the inclination came to me. Working in this way, also allowed me to connect with some fabulous people who were living here and doing similar things to me. Bali had become a little hub for entrepreneurs, taking time out to work on a special project, or like me, simply run an online business from Bali. I found out about these cool co-working spaces that were scattered around Bali. A place for people to come and share a work space for a little while or a long while.

I mixed things up a bit, as I wasn't so keen on getting stuck in any sort of routine. Sometimes I would jump on a scooter with my laptop and spend a few hours working from one of these places, other times I would take my laptop down to the beach, other times I would sit on the deck of my villa and write. But one of the things I found I really did enjoy was spending time with other people. There had been that part of me that was reluctant to connect with others. I think this was related to the guilt I felt at leaving Simon, almost like, if I could not find joy with him and I loved him so much, then I shouldn't allow myself to find joy with other people. But I knew this was a belief that was limiting me, and I really enjoyed talking to new people, having a laugh, sharing ideas about life and forming new friendships.

I suppose this was not one of the things I was looking for, nor really expecting during my year of living joyfully, part of me felt it was going to be a solitary experience for some reason. But it was proving to provide the space for some wonderful friendships to develop.

I met Liv at one of the co-working spaces. Her and her hubby had a graphic design and multimedia online business. They had been travelling for almost twelve months and had been in Bali for about two months. We just seemed to click and spent quite a bit of time together, as she was living in a similar area to me and she started to come along to Georgia's yoga classes.

As her and her hubby's year of travel was coming to an end, they were heading home to Sydney for Christmas, which coincided with the time I had to leave to get my new visa. I had played around with the idea of heading to Hawaii to spend Christmas with my Dad, Tabitha and little Zac but something in me told me that I needed to keep moving forward and while my time in Hawaii turned out to be a wonderful experience, I didn't really want to be taken back into the space where I had done so much of my healing. I wasn't convinced it would be a joyful experience.

And so, when Liv asked me if I had thought about going to Australia and if I would like to spend Christmas with them, my heart gave a little jump. I felt a bubble of excitement welling inside of me. Australia was so close to Bali that I had played around with the idea over the last six months, but I knew Sydney was also a big busy city and I wasn't sure it would allow me the same freedom and flow I was being afforded here in Bali.

Liv and Tom lived in Bondi and had been leasing out their unit for the last year. And as Liv explained to me, the way to manage Sydney was to simply do it your own way. You could quite easily slip into the busy craziness of the city or you could cultivate a pretty simple life just doing what you wanted. There was much on offer, and you could choose to dive into it as much or as little as you wished.

Maybe I hadn't just met Liv when I did by chance.

Liv and Tom left a week before I did, which allowed them time to resettle into their home before I joined them. They were so welcoming in having me stay with them. It was a simple, easy arrangement. It worked for them and worked for me and it would work for as long as it was supposed to.

I was giddy with excitement when I landed in Sydney. It was hot, being the middle of summer, and busy and big, but I liked it. I liked the energy that was in the air. When I arrived in Bondi, I started buzzing on another level. It had its own feel, its own identity, one that I felt say: You have permission to be here and do what you want, anything goes.

I woke up early my first morning and wandered down to the beach to watch the sun rise. I sat on the grass, staring out to yet another new horizon. I didn't know what lay on this horizon for me. I felt such peace and acceptance within me. Wherever this goes, I trusted was exactly where I needed to go. My intention I shared with the Universe as I sat there watching the sun gently start to dance on the ocean, was simply to continue to live a life that was one of joy. That I continued to have the courage to live my life how I wanted, and not by any other rules. That I was guided to the joy that I knew the Universe was creating for me. That I had the awareness and centeredness to hear the inner voice telling me gently how to navigate the path before me, when to pause, when to turn, when to change.

I trusted that the Universe would remind me to stop

and breathe and come back to me and create the 'there' that I knew I was able to find while I was here. I knew I could do this. I had created it with the help of a snowy mountain once many years ago, I had created it with the help of my friend Snow, for too many years, I had created it with the help of my beautiful unborn baby girl and I had created it for myself over the last six months.

I had done it. I had found that place in Bali, all by myself. Now, I knew that I could create that life and find my there anywhere, because it was here. It was within me. It always was and it always will be, it is always there for me to access and it will always be there for me to access. I just had to remember how. And I had remembered. I was so proud of myself. I had done it. I had gone home.

I made a promise to myself as I watched the sunrise over Bondi Beach, that I would never forget that home is always within me. I just had to choose it.

And as the rising sun became one with the ocean—a sole surfer paddled into the golden path that danced on top of the water and he suddenly became one with the sun and the ocean—I had never seen anything more beautiful in my whole life. As the tears ran from my eyes in pure joy, I remembered that there is no separation. We are all one. And the beauty that I was witnessing in the coming together of the sun, water and surfer, was simply a reflection of the divine beauty that was within me.

I was part of that.

I was that.

Suddenly, I got it and the world around me looked

different.

Home was within me, and I was part of everything around me, and therefore home is everywhere. I realised that no matter where or what I was doing, how I was doing it, none of it mattered because I would always be home.

I was home.

When I was in light I was there. When I was in darkness I was there. When I am in light I will be there and even if I am in darkness I will still be there. Everything had been perfect, after all. Home is simply whatever *is*: The good and the bad. The happy and the sad. The flow and the struggle. The freedom and the restriction. The faith and the doubt. The light and the dark.

I wandered home, with my head in the clouds and my feet firmly planted on the ground.

I was there while I was here and I could never not be again.

FINDING HOME

I ran into the yoga class that evening straight from the surf, my hair still wet, the salt still sitting on my skin and the high of catching my first waves zipping through me. I breathed deeply as I hit my mat, full of gratitude for arriving and for whatever this practice would bring to me. I wasn't sure if my being could handle too much more fullness, that is exactly how I was feeling. Completely full.

Full of life.

Full of gratitude.

Full of excitement.

Full of wonderment.

Full of freedom.

Full of joy.

I had been in an incredible euphoric, introspective

yet completely externally focused state all day. It was a strangely unique feeling yet it was also quite familiar and I was enjoying its presence, but at the same time I didn't mind if it left me, because I knew it was always there to return to me whenever I wanted to find it, it couldn't disappear. I had made it so hard, when it was so simple.

As I began my practice, my body moved in flow with my breath, in complete harmony with my whole being. I was connected deeply with my inner self and all that was around me.

I flowed within this euphoric state pose after pose. As I moved into another pose, I felt a hand gently connect with my ankle and my lower back. I knew it must have been the teacher guiding my body deeper into the pose, but as it connected with me, my whole being jolted like it had been shocked by an electric current. I knew he felt it too, because his hand quickly but gently released itself from my body. I was momentarily frazzled and thrown off balance, physically and mentally, but I steadied my body and silenced my curious mind and returned my focus inward and back into my flow.

∞

I noticed her when she came into the class. How could I not? She was shining. She was just so incredibly alive. Now, it is not like she is the first attractive woman to walk into this yoga room. This is Bondi, home to many beautiful people, however none have ever caught my eye like she did.

Her hair was wet and hanging down her back. She looked like she had literally just jumped from the surf and run up the street. It was her presence that was most compelling, there was a deep sense of calm and peace and a lightness that seemed to permeate through her cells.

Once we began the practice, my mind was totally focussed on guiding each person in that room through a beautiful experience. That was my role to play as an instructor, to guide the practice. Sometimes I would assist those in the class to go deeper into a pose, by guiding their physical body, and that is what I did with her. I did not recall that it was her, because the class was so full and my mind had released any thoughts of her specifically, until I touched her and then I felt her.

I felt the energy of the connection between us and her body shudder in response. I allowed myself to pull away but it felt like a strong magnetic hold and as I released, my inner voice screamed, *No, don't let go*.

Yoga was all about letting go and I had trained myself to masterfully silence my mind and centre my focus. So, I let go of that strange moment and returned my focus to my class.

∞

Pose after pose, my body moved with such grace and flow. I felt like I was on another planet. Never had I moved with such power and ease through a yoga class.

And as I moved into my shavasana, I welcomed the feel of the mat beneath my body and I allowed myself to ground into the moment. I smiled as I could feel my cells smiling and I felt a deep joy radiating from my soul. My yoga practice had brought me to this place of stillness, calm and joy, and I knew that on some parallel level, my whole life experience had brought me to this place and this moment in time. I melted into the mat, all thoughts leaving me, all feelings leaving me and I felt nothing but a huge golden light surrounding me and I allowed myself to witness it swirling with a powerful gentleness around my body.

∞

I quietly moved from person to person, as they lay in their shavasana, placing eye pillows over their eyes and lightly spraying a midst of essential oils over their resting body. When I came to her, I was overcome by her presence once again. She lay there with an almost cheeky smile on her face, like the little child who finds the lolly jar when no one else can find it. She had a stillness to her that was both beautiful and deeply compelling. As I placed the eye pillow over her eyes, I was drawn to her. As I placed my fingertips on her temple and I felt myself become one with her, I silently moaned as I remembered. I remembered this and I remembered her.

And while I desperately wanted to stay in that space with her, I knew that I did not need to force life, for when you let go and trust in life, it creates that which you desire. I listened when my inner voice told me to walk away and allow her this moment, I respected my wisdom and I respected her experience. This was her experience. This was her life. She had somehow returned to me; the Universe had created this moment for me. It was a profound moment. We had found one another again. Yet, I would not force life and if she was to stand at the end of this class and walk away and I was never to see her again, I would know that this was what our souls were to experience.

I removed my fingers from her temple, and returned to my own space, I felt like I had been transported to another reality. It was different than that which I had momentarily felt with her, but it was my reality, one which I had crafted and one which I was able to find my own sense of fulfilment, peace and stillness. It was my bliss and I had created it after years of stumbling through life.

I had found my path and I had finally come together within myself after a deeply powerful healing experience in Bali a couple of years ago. I was on a Yoga retreat, escaping yet another failed relationship and desperate to find my way in life and break my old patterns. I didn't have a clue how I was going to do this, but somehow the Universe intervened and the most extraordinarily beautiful and powerful soul came into my life.

She, was doing the same yoga retreat and had come from the other side of the world, but I knew our paths crossing at that time was in some way *divinely* created. We were seated beside one another one night during dinner and I found myself sharing my story with her. She evoked such a strong sense of trust that my deepest truths and darkest failings spilled from me. She held space like no one I had ever met before. I didn't know at this stage, that she was, in her own unique way, a gifted and powerful healer.

As we left dinner and returned to our rooms, she grabbed my hand and while she looked a little hesitant and slightly uncomfortable at overstepping some unspoken boundary, she asked me to meet her at the beach at sunrise, as she felt compelled to assist me to release my old stuff and find freedom.

I know this was not why she had come on this retreat, it was meant to be about time for her and her own growth, but I sensed, as she obviously had too, that we had come together for her to guide me through this and onto my path once again.

I am still not completely sure what happened that next morning as the sun rose on a new day. But whatever magic transpired in that space, she changed me, she changed my soul and she changed my life. I think of her as my Mystery Angel, she was all knowing and all seeing. An Angel of such beauty and grace who was dropped into my life at just the right time.

I left Bali with so much understanding about my connection to the young spirited girl who had come into my life all those years ago in a bar in the snow. I understood my deep old connection to her soul and why our union that extraordinary night had transformed my life. I understood why I had spent years desperately searching for something or someone who could take me back to that place that I went with her. And I healed it. I healed my soul story with her and I released her soul and I released my soul from hers. From then on, I worked at carving a new soul story, one where I was enough within myself without her, one where I could find that place, that incredible feeling within myself. Now, I had been able to do that.

I loved the life that I had created for myself and deep within, I knew that I had created this moment too. This moment where *she* lay on a yoga mat, in my yoga studio. But how I managed the moments to follow this would determine what my next chapter was too look like.

As I sat in silence with my *self* before finishing the class, I felt so much love for her and so much joy for her, because I knew that she had made it too. I could feel that extraordinary place that she had discovered within herself as I shared it with her once again, albeit for just a moment in time.

And my heart and soul was in complete acceptance of what was to be, would be.

∞

As he placed the eye pillow over my eyes and placed his fingertips on my temples I did not react with shock as

I had previously. Instead, I felt him merge into my light and we became one, just like the sun that met the ocean that morning. It was the most natural and profoundly beautiful assimilation of two energies into one. I did not flinch, I did not fight it, I did not question it. I allowed it and it felt heart-achingly Divine. I allowed his energy to be one with mine, my soul remembered. I remembered his touch. I remembered his soul. I remembered being one with him. I remembered it all and my soul laughed.

Well played Universe! Well played!

As he gently removed his fingers from my temple, I felt his energy release from mine as he moved away from me. But I did not crave it like once I did, because now I returned home. That divine place that I had found within myself and it didn't feel lonely, it didn't feel lacking, it didn't feel frightening. It was home and what I had with him there in that moment, I had here in this moment. Because I chose to come back and my *self* held all that I needed.

I remained in my shavasana for as long as my soul told me to stay. I heard the external guidance gently bringing others around me back into their reality and felt the movement of energy around me, as others packed up and left the space. And still my being could not disconnect from the mat below me and still my soul insisted that I stay in this moment.

Who was I to fight it? I trusted it implicitly. I don't know how long I stayed there … it may have only been a few extra minutes, it may have been much longer and when I sat up, he was sitting there on his mat patiently waiting for me. *How many lifetimes had he waited patiently for me to reach this point?*

'Hey.'

'Hey?' His, eyes were twinkling. 'Long time no see.'

And then we laughed. And the invisible tension that was hanging in the air between us, dissipated into the night, into eternity. I moved to sit in front of him.

'So, how are you?'

'Amazing,' I laughed knowing that I had finally made it. 'I made it *home*!'

He laughed with me as he nodded and understood, 'How was it for you?'

'It's been some ride,' I paused in contemplation. 'But I did it. I made it back this time around.'

I looked at him deeply for the first time, and my soul moaned in silence, a deep aching release of lifetimes of pain and struggle.

'And now you are here.'

'Yep, and now you are here.'

His gaze matched my wonderment in the divine play of the Universe.

∞

'Hey Gorgeous One'

'Hey, sweet girl! You found each other, didn't you?'

'How can you possibly know that! But, yes, we did! It was Crazy. Divine. Amazing!'

'Love it. Just Perfect!'

'How come you didn't tell me you had met him in Bali on your yoga retreat? How come you didn't tell me you knew?'

'I didn't know straight away that you were the girl from his past, nor that he was that guy in snow. The pieces didn't fall into place. I kind of forget most things when I work with people, you know that. But after your huge soul story session, it did link together for me, but I knew that it wasn't my place to say anything, it was not my story to tell. If I had said anything to you it would have interfered with the flow of what was destined to be, when you found your way home. And, see how magically it all came together once you had done your work.'

'Yes, I know!'

'You've got to do your work.'

'And I did!'

'Yep, you certainly did. And in finding home, you found him. Enjoy the reunion gorgeous one, and give him my love.'

THE END

ACKNOWLEDGEMENTS

To mum and dad for gifting me with this life, and lovingly guiding me to be uniquely me and encouraging me to share the best version of me with the world, without expectation of what that looks like. You kept it simple and real, allowing me to have my feet firmly on the ground, and my head in the clouds just enough to dream.

Dad, you were the story teller, never able to get to the end of a story without muffling it with your laughter. Oh, how I miss that laugh – and your stories. You passing from this life was one of my greatest gifts, for it lead me to waking up and remembering why I am gracing this world this time around.

Mum, your love of books instilled my passion for writing. You lovingly typed my stories on your typewriter, so I could transform them into books, and it was in that little girl that the dream to one day write my own book was born. And here she is. May she take pride of place on your bookshelf after you have read and re-read her on the back deck.

Mary, Brigid and Kevin we were blessed with a childhood of love and grounding simplicity. And with each other. We do family beautifully and I love yours like they are mine and I treasure what we have created. Thank you for loving me, with all my quirks and nuances.

Maria and Sara, as you know I was the girl with no friends, too shy to connect to others and content to be the observer of life, it felt safer there. You girls saw me beneath the painfully shy exterior, and made it safe enough for me to ditch the protection of my cocoon and find my wings. Life and children and writing books and all those things get in the way of spending time together, yet you are always in my heart and I am forever grateful for our souls dancing together in this life.

To my wonder women, Sara, Emily and Patrice, I thank you for lovingly supporting me with your healing gifts, through my own journey home.

To Glen, your patience during my growth tantrums has been invaluable. Thank you for keeping me focussed on becoming more me and sharing that with the world, albeit slowly at times.

To my clients, you are my inspiration for writing. I learn so much from each one of you and I thank you for trusting me to support and guide you. For those of you who showed me aspects of Halia's story, through your own experiences, I am so grateful to you for subconsciously reassuring me that this book had to be written and I was on the right path. To Sally Rust, I worked with you the day I downloaded Let's Go Home and I was guided to invade your treatment and ask you questions about the story. You knew the story I had received that morning, and that freaked us both out, yet affirmed to me that this story had to be told and there was a pushy and powerful energy at play, insistent on me being the writer.

And to the gorgeous Katie Dean, my everlasting gratitude to you for guiding me to the most extraordinary editor, the beautiful Natasha Gilmour.

Lara Lupish, my amazing creative friend, thank you for believing in me and Let's Go Home during our first netball sideline conversation. You pulled your team of superstars together to transform me into the author you saw me to be and encouraged me to present her to the world, and I am so grateful for your generosity and support.

Karen McDermott, from Making Magic Happen Academy, thank you landing in my sphere at just the right time and helping me to bring my book to the world.

Natasha Gilmour, where do I begin? As my editor, you crafted Let's Go Home into the book it was meant to be. I may have put the words on paper, but it was you who diligently danced with them so they flowed and took Halia and her story to another level. You took me by the hand and guided me through the publishing process, never doubting this book or me as an author. For this I am full of gratitude.

Your connection to Halia and her story, and your unwavering belief that it is a story worth sharing with the world, has kept me completely connected to my vision. I thank your beautiful soul for being my birth partner, as I birth my book into the world. It has been a long and divine labour, and a beautiful friendship and wonderful soul connection has been cultivated in the process. This has been the unexpected gift in bringing Let's Go Home into the world.

Kokoda, Lucia and Xavier, you are as excited about this book being published as I am. You have been with me every step of the way. You slept in the early morning hours while I diligently and joyfully wrote and on waking, after a quick kiss and cuddle, you respectfully gave me that extra half hour or so in my writing zone, to continue to draw through the words that you all believed would one day be 'Mummy's first book'. You are my most divine creations and I love you more than any words could say. Always know this and feel it in your heart, because it is, and will always be there for you.

And to you Luke, my love. My life is better because of you. You love, respect and 'get' me like no other and because of that this whole life thing is so much more doable, and joyful. I couldn't do it with anyone else, because I don't think anyone else would allow me to be as me as you do. I am eternally grateful that we chose each other for this life, and I've got this feeling we are nailing it, dancing the dance in perfect harmony.

And finally, thank you Halia for choosing me to tell your story. You made writing your story the easiest thing I have ever done. You turned publishing your story into a lesson for me in trust, patience, non-attachment, surrender and a little more trust. From that Saturday morning in April 2016 when you landed in my consciousness until now, as I write this, you have been an intriguing and powerful presence. You have pushed me to step into aspects of myself, that have been waiting for the opportunity to rise. You forced me to step into my power and move outside my comfort zone. You taught me to listen and surrender. You taught me to believe in myself as a writer and as an author. You believed in me and I believe in you, your story and why we must share it with others, so that they may be inspired to change, to look deeper within and find their way home.

To you my reader, as you connect with Halia, may you find the seed that she has interwoven in her words, and may it guide you home to who you really are.